"Do you never sl..."

Having thought... paused for a mome... was just about to go up to bed, my lord," she replied, "I was not aware that you were still here," she added tartly.

Barrisford chuckled. "No, I realize you did not. Did I startle you?"

"Of course not. My heart always races like this."

He had risen from his place in the shadows, and he moved closer to her as he spoke.

"Does it indeed?" he inquired gently. "That doesn't sound at all healthy, Lady Rosemary."

She opened her mouth to speak, but he put a finger over her lips and she subsided. She was keenly aware of the gentle pressure of his fingers and the intent way in which he was studying her. She did not meet his eyes until a minute had passed and he suddenly cupped his hand beneath her chin and lifted it.

"Look above you, Lady Rosemary," he whispered. They were once more under the kissing bough, and seeing that, she felt her knees beginning to grow weak, for his intentions were evident. Folding her close to him, he again pressed his lips against hers, this time with a firm but gentle kiss. The faint scent of lime clung to him, and she knew suddenly that for the rest of her life, whenever she encountered that fragrance, she would remember this moment. Without her willing it, her arms slipped around his neck and she responded with all the ardor of a newly awakened passion.

A Christmas Betrothal

Mona Gedney

ZEBRA BOOKS
KENSINGTON PUBLISHING CORP.

ZEBRA BOOKS are published by

Kensington Publishing Corp.
475 Park Avenue South
New York, NY 10016

First Printing: November, 1993

Printed in the United States of America

One

It all began one dark November night when John Arthur Trevelyan, the fifth Duke of Stedham, found that he had at last done what his critics had long predicted. For generations, the Trevelyans had been noted for their reckless ways and their careless charm, and Jack Trevelyan, the present duke, was no exception. There were some, in fact, who said that he was the very image of the first duke, who had accompanied the Merry Monarch home to England in 1660 and had been rewarded for both his loyalty and his charming company with a new title. Unlike many of the Cavaliers, he had not only regained his own lands, but had also been awarded additional ones as well. Not all of his descendants had shared his extraordinary talent for attracting good luck, however. The present duke, after a most unfortunate evening at the gaming tables, had just spent a grim afternoon reviewing his financial affairs with his man of business. That long-suffering gentleman had turned a deaf ear to the duke's repeated assurances that they could "bring the thing about."

"You have nothing left to bring about, Your Grace," said Mr. Crispin bluntly, determined to make his point. "You have avoided looking at your accounts anytime this past five years and we must have plain pound dealing now. After you reclaim your voucher from last night's gambling, you will have nothing left to draw upon—not even enough to continue the upkeep of Marston Hall."

"You are too pessimistic, Crispin," returned the duke cheerfully, although he was a little startled by his retainer's directness. "Sell off a bit of land. That will do the trick, will it not?"

Crispin straightened his narrow shoulders and cleared his throat. "I can't wrap it up in clean linen, Your Grace. You have no Trevelyan land left to sell. Everything belonging to you now is entailed and must go to your heir." He stared earnestly at the elegant figure before him, and, fearful that his warning would once again be lightly dismissed, he added abruptly, "You have no disposable property of any value left except your stables and the jewelry your wife left to your daughters."

His attention fully engaged now, Stedham turned to face Crispin directly. "And what of the Funds?" he demanded. "What of my investments there?"

"Gone, Your Grace," Crispin replied simply.

"Do you recall the wagers with Colonel Picket and the other gentlemen over the bout between Gentleman Jim and the blacksmith from Orkney?"

Stedham nodded, his eyes darkening as he remembered that other unfortunate wager. He had been so certain that the blacksmith would win that he had indiscreetly bet against the odds. The results had been disastrous.

"You told me then to do whatever was necessary to pay your debt of honor, even though I told you at the time that you must not continue dipping into your principal. And then you ordered new apparel for your daughters, as well as for all of the relatives who reside with them at Marston Hall. Then Lady Rosemary wrote to you and told you that the roof in the west wing was leaking and you had that redone. The constant upkeep of that establishment is very costly, Your Grace. After that there came the new string of hunters you purchased at Tattersall's. And then you had me pay the debts of young Royalton on top of all that."

It was clear that Crispin intended to continue his list indefinitely, but the duke cut him short. "Of course I had you pay his debts. The silly young cub was going to put a period to his existence. Thought he couldn't face the world if he couldn't pay his losses. It was no great thing to help him."

"But, Your Grace," said Crispin patiently,

"you were in no position to help him. In fact, helping him simply brought about your own ruin more quickly."

Stedham glanced up sharply at this. "And so that is the truth of the matter, is it, Crispin? I am not just in deep water? I am indeed ruined?"

Crispin nodded his head and watched unhappily as the duke sank into a chair before the fire. It brought him no pleasure to force this news upon Stedham. Despite his infuriating habit of ignoring Crispin's own sound advice, as well as that of his banker and his solicitor, it was impossible to dislike the duke. Although he was self-indulgent and careless, he was also kindly and openhanded to a fault, unwilling to allow another to be in distress if he could remedy the matter. Stedham was not at all self-sacrificing, but if a problem could be solved by the application of a little money, he had always been very willing to undertake it. Such an attitude had long endeared him to those whose pockets were frequently to let, but it had caused his critics to wag their heads knowingly, predicting that sooner or later he would be brought to grief through his own gambling and his thoughtless generosity.

"We *could* sell your horses, Your Grace," said Crispin, attempting to sound an optimistic note in the face of Stedham's unwontedly grim expression. "And, as I said, there is the jewelry that Lady Stedham left to your daughters."

Stedham shook his head. "No, Crispin," he replied shortly. "That is out of the question. I won't take that from my girls, even though I appear to be taking the roof from over their heads. Besides," he added, a wry smile twisting the corners of his mouth, "from what you have told me, their trinkets would be no more than a drop in the bucket, so there is no heroism in my sparing them that."

He sat silently for a moment, then waved Crispin toward the door. "There is nothing more that you can do for me, Crispin," he said briefly. Then, glancing at his retainer's despondent expression, Stedham attempted a rallying tone and added more gently, "You have done what you can on my behalf. I know that and I am grateful. Perhaps we can meet tomorrow and decide what is best to be done."

Glad to see a little of his master's habitual optimism, Crispin replied in a voice far more positive than his mood warranted. "Just so, Your Grace. After a good night's sleep we will see what can be managed. I will come to you tomorrow afternoon."

Stedham nodded and Crispin bowed himself out of the room, his mind already busy with possibilities that might spare his master for a few more days.

The duke had been engaged to spend the evening with friends and Baxter, his valet, ventured into the library to remind him of that fact. He was dismissed with a wave of the hand

9

and an unusually curt request to be left in peace. Baxter withdrew silently, but lingered close by, waiting to see if he might be of service.

Stedham had never faced an unpleasant situation in his life, always leaving domestic problems to his wife and financial ones to Crispin. After Lady Stedham's death ten years earlier, his oldest daughter, Lady Rosemary, had assumed that burden. The duke sat long before the fire that night, his none-too tender conscience troubled by the thought that this disaster would also put a period to any hope of establishing his four daughters in creditable marriages.

Indeed, he had heretofore given very little thought to the matter. Good-natured and easygoing though he was, he was not a domestic man, and contented himself by sending occasional gifts to Marston Hall whenever he happened to recall that he had a family. He had blithely ignored the fact that Rosemary had not yet had a season in London, comforting himself with the notion that as soon as he got his affairs in order he would make it up to her. Indeed, she had told him herself that she could not consider leaving Marston Hall for so long a time while her sisters needed her care. Now two of the others were also of an age to be married. Indeed, it seemed to him that all that he had left in the way of capital were his four daughters.

When Baxter entered the library some hours later, he found the room in darkness and his master staring into the golden glow of the fire.

"Gone up in flames, Baxter," the duke muttered, moving the fire screen to kick an escaping coal back into the heart of the blaze. "My whole life, gone up in flames."

For once, Baxter did not reprove his master for such cavalier treatment of his shining boots. Instead, he watched that gentleman with a troubled gaze. He had been Stedham's valet since the days of that lord's scapegrace, heedless youth, and never before had Baxter seen him at a standstill.

Clearing his throat, he attempted to speak cheerfully to Stedham. "May I bring you something, Your Grace? Or perhaps you would feel a little more yourself if you changed and went out for dinner."

When Stedham did not respond, Baxter decided to risk reminding him of his dinner engagement. "You were engaged to meet Lord Findlay at nine o'clock, and he sent a footman to ask if you were still planning to join him later this evening."

Stedham stood as though he had heard nothing, but Baxter, encouraged by the fact that he had not been told to take himself about his business and wishing to distract his master's attention from his troubled thoughts, ventured to add, "Mr. Aubrey Townsend stopped earlier and left his card, Your Grace. Fleetwood told him that you were engaged, and he said that he would call again tomorrow."

Stedham's head jerked up at the mention of Townsend's name. "My heir came to call, did he?" he inquired bitterly. "I suppose he wished to see if I am taking proper care of the estates he looks forward to inheriting—and to see, of course, if I am looking in good health."

Baxter was caught off guard by his master's tone. He was aware of Crispin's visit and knew, of course, that Stedham always sailed close to the wind, so he had not expected the duke to be in a pleasant frame of mind, but this was far worse than he had looked for. It was true that the wealthy Mr. Townsend was seldom seen in Stedham Place, but that was partially because he was very young and had spent most of his time away at school. It was also true that when he was in London on holiday, his farsighted mama was careful to keep him out of the duke's orbit, not wishing her son to acquire that gentleman's careless habits. It had also occurred to the careful Mrs. Townsend that Lord Stedham was not above touching her son for a loan since all of the property would one day be his, and she had forestalled this possibility neatly by limiting her son's contact to an occasional brief Christmas visit—under her strict chaperonage—to pay his respects to the duke. Never before, however, had Baxter heard Stedham refer to Townsend in anything other than a rather amused, offhanded manner.

"I believe, my lord," said Baxter, choosing his words carefully, "that Mr. Townsend merely wished to pay his respects, having just returned from his trip to Italy."

He watched his master closely, waiting for a response, but none was forthcoming. "Fleetwood and I were saying that he seems a very pleasant young gentleman, Your Grace," he offered hopefully.

Stedham, suddenly struck by a new thought, poked the edges of the fire absently. "Yes, I suppose he is quite pleasant, Baxter. I was too harsh. And he is young—and impressionable."

"Just so, Your Grace," he said eagerly, pleased to see Stedham looking slightly less grim. "And I'm sure that he will be back tomorrow. Now, if you like, I will lay out your evening clothes and send John around to tell Lord Findlay that you will join him shortly."

Stedham's expression had grown steadily more cheerful. "By all means, Baxter. Offer him my apologies and say that I will be with him directly."

Greatly relieved by this return to normal behavior, Baxter bowed and hurried away to dispatch John and to prepare his lordship's raiment. He would have felt less optimistic, however, had he been privy to Stedham's thoughts as that gentleman planned his course of action.

In an unusually thoughtful frame of mind, the duke joined Lord Findlay and a party of friends and allowed himself to be severely taken to task for being so late.

"What kept you so long, Stedham?" demanded one of the party, a portly gentleman with a florid complexion. "We had dinner held back a full thirty minutes waiting for you. It wasn't fit to eat by the time it arrived at table!"

The dark-eyed man seated next to him winked at Stedham. "And one glance at Raxton would tell you that he wasted away to skin and bone while he waited. Why, he is a mere shadow of his former self."

Ignoring the laughter of the others, the maligned Raxton drew himself up, endeavoring fruitlessly to look a little less like a plump pouter pigeon and hoping desperately that his corset would not creak. "No matter what certain vulgar persons choose to tell you, Stedham, the hot buttered crab was *cold* when it arrived at table! It would have been absolutely barbaric to eat it in such a state. There was no choice but to send it back again." Feeling that he had made his point, Raxton sank back into his chair, allowing himself to breathe again.

Before anyone else could make another remark that would set him off, Stedham hastened to offer his apologies to Findlay and to all of his guests. There was not a one in this dissipated group, he reflected with an inward smile, of whom Mrs. Amelia Townsend would approve. Indeed, her low opinion of Stedham, well known to that gentleman, would be confirmed by this collection of roués and rakes.

"My heir dropped by this evening," he said casually, failing to mention that he had not actually seen young Townsend and leaving the impression that this unexpected visit was what had held him up. "He has turned out rather well, I believe," he added, glancing at the faces of the others to note their reactions.

Raxton nodded judiciously. "Saw him when he came down from Oxford last Christmas. He was visiting the clubs with Barrisford The boy is not so handsome as his uncle, but he will do very well. Hope he is not so high in the instep as that devil Barrisford, though. The fellow gave me the cut direct when I offered to have a simple game of whist with the boy."

"And I can't imagine why Barrisford failed to encourage his cub of a nephew to take up with a gamester like you, Raxton," said Henry Sayers, his dark eyes laughing. "You should be grateful that Barrisford did nothing more than turn his back on you. A man with a short temper and a fine aim is no one to be trifled with."

Raxton shuddered delicately as he envisioned the possibilities suggested by this remark and wiped his forehead with a lacy handkerchief. "That is not a matter for jest, Sayers. Not even Barrisford would have called me out over such a matter as that. Dueling is just not done anymore. Moreover, it's against the law."

"Not fleecing the youngster must have disappointed you greatly, Raxton," observed Lord Findlay lazily. "I understand that young Townsend is a very wealthy prize. Even though he does not receive control of his entire estate until his marriage, he has access to more money now than most of us will see in a lifetime. It seems unkind that you could not have shared at least a portion of it."

"Well, of course, it does," agreed Raxton, pleased to see that someone took such an imminently sensible view of the situation. "Although I confess that I would prefer to have my dealings with him after he marries."

"It was quite farsighted of her husband to see to it that the boy has a powerful incentive for breaking with Amelia," said Findlay. "No doubt she will make it as difficult for him as possible. I fear, Raxton," he said to his friend, "that by the time you are allowed close to him, your pigeon will not be quite so easy to pluck."

Stedham picked up Findlay's silver snuffbox and studied it, hoping that his questions would seem casual. "Is he really so inexperienced, then?" inquired Stedham carelessly. "I would

16

have thought that, being Barrisford's nephew, he would be up to every rig in town."

"Surely you do not forget that Amelia Townsend is his mother, my dear Stedham," returned Sayers, another gentleman addicted to gaming. "She has supervised his every movement very carefully. Far be it from her to allow the boy a little breathing space. The good lady may consider herself an invalid, but she could scarcely be more active in her son's behalf if she were hale and hearty."

Sayers paused and studied his immaculate nails thoughtfully. "I was fully as hopeful as Raxton here that I would have an opportunity to join the lad in a quiet evening of cards once he was no longer a scruffy schoolboy, but as soon as he arrived in London last spring, she packed him off to the Continent with a tutor." He sighed. "It was a grievous disappointment, but I must hope that now he is back in town another opportunity will present itself. One must always be hopeful."

"Perhaps he is more in the petticoat line," offered Stedham. "He *is*, after all, a fine-looking young man—and a wealthy one. He must hold a great appeal for the ladies."

Findlay, momentarily aroused from his lethargy, raised his glass to regard his friend closely. "Stedham! Have you been attending to what we has been said? We are speaking of Amelia Townsend's son! Can you imagine her allowing a son of hers to be exposed to such temptation? After all," he added slyly, "she has kept him out of your path rather neatly."

Stedham smiled pleasantly. "So she has. I can't imagine that she could have been with him every minute, however. As Sayers said, she is something of an invalid."

"No need for her to be with him every minute," Raxton assured him knowledgeably. "If she ain't with him, though, that tutor is—or worse yet, Barrisford! No chance to get at the boy at all."

Stedham, although never fond of Amelia, mentally saluted her careful protection of her son. Her late husband, a very distant relative of the duke, had been his heir, and now her only son, Aubrey Townsend, would one day be the sixth Duke of Stedham. It was no secret that she did not regard that prospect with pleasure. She had indeed been heard to say that the title would bring her son nothing but moth-eaten estates that had been allowed to go to rack and ruin and a cataract of debts. Since the death of her husband, she had been determined to protect him from fortune hunters, including Stedham in their number. It had been a matter of annoyance to him in the past, when it would have been quite convenient to be able to borrow from the boy for repairs to property that would one day be his, but now Stedham could see clearly that Amelia's zealous protection had been a godsend.

"I am afraid, Sayers, that you may not reel

in your fat fish after all," said the duke, smiling. "I should imagine that there are a good many matchmaking mamas who will plan their campaigns to attract Townsend's attention quite as carefully as any general. If he has an eye for the ladies, I am afraid you may be outflanked."

Sayers nodded in agreement. "I watched several attempts last spring—and it was really most amusing. Townsend does seem very susceptible to beauty when he is out from under his mama's thumb, for within a week's time I saw him making one in the court of three different young lovelies—and each of them was, of course, inclined to smile upon him."

"But nothing came of any of them?" demanded Stedham anxiously.

Sayers raised one shoulder languidly. "But of course not, my dear Stedham. Mama Townsend might have been ill, but her spies told her everything and she snatched away her boy before any harm could be done." He touched his moustache thoughtfully. "Quite a masterful lady. Had she been with Wellington, our war would have been over in half the time."

When Stedham returned to his home in the early hours of the following morning, he did not go immediately to his bedchamber as he normally did. Instead, he again closeted himself in the darkened library, having ordered John to make the fire up again and to tell Baxter not to wait up for him any longer. His valet, disconcerted by this unaccountable behavior, ignored the footman's message and maintained a vigil outside the door of the library, discreetly out of sight should Stedham suddenly leave the room. Even though his master had consented to going out, Baxter had not been able to rid himself of the feeling that something was very wrong. Such odd behavior as this confirmed his suspicions.

After waiting for almost an hour with no sign of life from within the library, Baxter could bear it no longer. Scratching discreetly at the door, he then entered quickly before the duke could send him away.

The duke was sitting in front of the fire, which had by now burned quite low, and at first he appeared unaware of his valet's presence.

"Excuse me, Your Grace," said Baxter gently. "I thought perhaps you might like for me to see you to your chamber. It is almost dawn, you know."

Stedham looked up at him, his face flushed, his eyes bright with excitement, his thoughts clearly elsewhere. Then, as he focused more clearly and recognized his servant, he smiled, looking almost jubilant. "Yes, I know, Baxter. There is no need to go to bed. I must go out in just an hour or two."

Baxter was shaken from his normal imperturbable manner. In all of his years of serving Stedham, he had never seen him greet the morning cheerfully. He had, in fact, seldom seen him greet the morning at all. He was a man inclined to stay up very late and to begin the day well past noon. "I beg your pardon, Your Grace," he said. "I thought for a moment that you said that you are waiting for the morning."

Stedham smiled again. "I did, Baxter. I have solved all of my problems and I need to settle some affairs as soon as possible."

Baxter, greatly relieved by his words, allowed himself a brief smile. "I am sure that I am glad to hear you say so, Your Grace. Would you be needing me to lay out your riding clothes for the morning?"

Stedham waved his hand carelessly. "It really makes no difference, Baxter. Choose whatever you think would do."

Baxter was at a loss. Stedham was normally very precise in his instructions about his wardrobe—and since Baxter had no idea what his master's morning activities would be, he had no idea what to select for him to wear. He watched Stedham, normally the most relaxed of men, rise from his chair and pace restlessly in front of the fire, nervously twisting the great square-cut emerald he always wore on his right hand.

Deciding that he would try one more time, Baxter cleared his throat tentatively. "Excuse me, Your Grace—"

Stedham turned to him and spoke, apparently unaware that his valet had said anything. "I have most certainly worked it out, Baxter! It is a master stroke, but I must have your help to carry out the matter."

"Indeed, Your Grace, anything that I could do—" stammered the valet, again caught off guard.

"Yes, I knew that I could count on you, Baxter," said the duke affectionately. "You have always stood by me, and I shall need you now. For you see, Baxter, I have determined that there is only one way in which my problem will be resolved."

"And what is that?" inquired his faithful servant, prepared to make a trip to the pawnshop with some valuable bauble belonging to the duke or to bear a letter to his banker.

Stedham stared down at the ring he had been twisting. "There is only one thing that will save us all, Baxter. It is time for me to die—and you must assist me."

Two

Marston Hall, home of the fifth Duke of Stedham, was a venerable establishment whose history dated back to the days of Elizabeth I. Indeed, the house itself was built in the shape of an E, thought to be a delicate compliment to that monarch, who visited there twice during the course of her reign. Its mellow red bricks and white quoins and cupolas were still as charming from a distance as they once were. It was only upon closer view that it became obvious that much of the brick was crumbling and that what had once been white was now much closer to gray.

Indeed, it took a small fortune simply to keep Marston Hall running. Not, of course, that it was kept in the manner it had been in former days. Now they kept the minimum number of servants and two of the wings were closed off completely. To say that the inhabitants lived on the proverbial shoestring would have been no more than the truth.

Nonetheless, it was still the scene of bustle and business, not only on rent days when the tenant farmers came to make their payments, but during the course of ordinary days as well. Part of the activity was supplied by the host of people who lived within its walls and part by their steady stream of callers, a scattering of them members of the nobility or the gentry, many of them countryfolk. The master of Marston Hall had never lived there since his childhood and had graced it with his presence only four times in the past ten years since his wife's death. It was much too far from town and revelry to suit his tastes. In the eyes of the countryside, Lady Rosemary Trevelyan, a young woman of only three-and-twenty, was the mistress of Marston Hall, and it was she to whom they came to pay their respects.

The lady in question surveyed the scene before her with a proprietary eye. The cavernous flagstoned kitchen of Marston Hall could scarcely have been busier. Mrs. O'Ryan, who now served as both cook and housekeeper for their more modest establishment after spending fifteen years as the housekeeper and supervisor of some thirty servants, was busy with her baking, and Cousin Merriweather had unfortunately taken it into her head that now would be the moment to fix a nourishing soup to take to old Mrs. Simms, one of their tenants. Merriweather was scarcely an accomplished cook and inclined in this, as in all things, to pause often in the process and inquire of those about her if she was doing the thing properly. Consequently, Mrs. O'Ryan was looking somewhat harried, a condition that was aggravated by the three small children gathered close about a nest of puppies beside the fire. With them were Isabella and Candace, two of Rosemary's younger sisters. Candace, a determined young girl of thirteen, had declared that the weather had turned too cold to leave the pups in the kennel and had established them securely in the kitchen, soothing Mrs. O'Ryan's protests as best she could.

"Besides, Mrs. O'Ryan," Candace was saying as she settled herself on a small stool next to the pups and picked one up with a businesslike air, "since we have to hand-feed some of them, this makes it much simpler. You know that Bella would catch her death if she went out in this weather."

Rosemary watched Candace's machinations in amusement. Her little sister was well aware that everyone loved the gentle Bella, who had already had one dangerous bout with an inflammation of the lungs the previous spring. There was no appeal more certain to win over the household to her way to seeing things.

"Oh, yes, indeed, Mrs. O'Ryan," chimed in Cousin Merriweather earnestly. "You know that dear Bella gets sick so easily. It is far better that the pups are in here if it will keep her from the cold." She stared doubtfully down at the kettle of soup she was stirring. "Do you think that Mrs. Simms would like some carrots in the soup or would they be too hard for her to digest? And perhaps I should add some fennel."

Mrs. O'Ryan, who was very fond of all of the children of the house, was not immune to such an appeal. She sniffed, giving in grudgingly. "Well, of course we must keep Lady Bella in health, but it doesn't seem right to have dogs in the kitchen of a duke, letting their hair fly all over everything."

Candace was aware that she had won her point, but she could not resist driving home her point. "And you know, Mrs. O'Ryan, that these are very special dogs. Uncle Webster told us that Sir Walter Scott has one just like these named Wallace."

Bella, whose gentle face had flushed when she became the subject of discussion, looked up from the tiny black morsel she was feeding and smiled. She was a quiet, dreamy girl, much addicted to the romances of the famous Scotsman.

"And it was so kind of Uncle Webster to bring Annie Laurie to us all the way from the Highlands," said Bella. "Why, he had to carry her with him all the way back to Marston Hall, and sit on top of the stagecoach in the most uncomfortable place so that she could stay with him."

Mrs. O'Ryan, clearly unimpressed by such

sacrifice on the part of Webster MacLean, an elderly and very distant relative of the late duchess, sniffed. "It would have been more to the good if he had brought you a dog that wasn't carrying a litter of young ones."

"Well, Uncle Webster didn't know that at the time, of course," said Candace, "but I think it is a splendid thing. Now we will have seven just like Annie Laurie."

Annie Laurie, the mother of the pups, had had a difficult time during their delivery, and she lay quietly now, her eyes closed, the pups, except for the two held by Bella and Candace, nestled close to her. Over them bent three children, Will, Charlotte, and Jamie, fascinated by their smallness. Apart from when they were sleeping, it was the first time that Rosemary could recall seeing all three children motionless at the same time. For a moment she wondered uneasily where the two older boys could be. It was unlike them to miss any new development in the household.

"And that is exactly what we need here," returned Mrs. O'Ryan dryly, "seven more mouths to feed." Looking up from pummeling the round of dough on the table before her, she caught Rosemary's warning glance, and her face reddened. Lady Rosemary did not encourage them to make reference to the fact that it was very difficult—not to say impossible—to make ends meet because of their very large household. She took her duties to the family very seriously. Her father was the head of the Trevelyan family and, as such, the one to whom they should be able to turn for help. Lady Rosemary considered herself his representative.

She and her three sisters had been joined by their spinster cousin, Merriweather Trevelyan, when Lady Stedham had died ten years earlier. Miss Trevelyan was to run the household and look after the girls, but, little by little, Lady Rosemary had taken over that role, although still appearing to defer to Cousin Merriweather By the time Rosemary was fifteen, she was looking after all of the business of the household and calling on the Trevelyan tenants on the estate. Everyone concerned had found this a satisfactory arrangement. Cousin Merriweather was constitutionally unable to make a decision; the very thought that she might make a mistake and upset someone gave her the headache and sent her to her room with her vinaigrette. Rosemary, on the other hand, thrived in the position of command, and she was a benevolent ruler, so those living within her realm were highly satisfied with the arrangement.

In fact, in the private opinion of Mrs. O'Ryan, who had stayed staunchly with them through it all, even when her salary had been greatly decreased and her duties greatly increased, Lady Rosemary had far too kind a heart. Over the years their household had acquired the elderly Webster MacLean, who ostensibly earned his keep by tutoring the children in history and languages, and the children of the late Lady Stedham's youngest sister, Jeanette Halleck, who had been left an impoverished widow with five active children, John, Robert, Will, Charlotte, and Jamie. Grief-stricken over her loss, Mrs. Halleck had faded quietly from this life, dying as quietly as she had lived, and leaving five children to be cared for.

Only last summer their ranks had swelled again with the arrival of two more maiden ladies from their father's family. Miss Marian Trevelyan and her twin sister Matilda had come, they said, for a brief stay. Their doctor had recommended a change of air after Matilda's illness and they had thought a country place like Marston Hall would provide just the sort of restful atmosphere they needed. They had arrived unexpectedly in August, and now, in December, they were showing no sign of leaving. Mrs. O'Ryan, like Lady Rosemary, suspected that they had come for good. Lady Rosemary suspected, too, that they had no other place to go.

When she had written a brief letter to her father, notifying him of their arrival and asking his permission for them to join the household permanently, he had carelessly agreed. To whom could they turn for help, he had written to Rosemary, if not to the head of their family?

"After all," Mrs. O'Ryan confided bitterly to the stew she was stirring after his response had arrived and Lady Rosemary had shared it with her, "why should he not agree to it? It's no skin off his nose if we have two more mouths to feed. We will have the same amount of household money and it is no trouble to him."

She would never have dared to voice such a thought to her mistress, for Lady Rosemary would have asked her what she would have her do with the elderly twins. "Would you have me send them to the poor farm, Mrs. O'Ryan?" she would have inquired, her direct gaze never wavering from the cook's eyes. Mrs. O'Ryan had learned her lesson with Webster MacLean, and she did not question Lady Rosemary's charitable decisions—at least not to her face. But she held long and heartfelt discussions with the pots and pans in the scullery, who never failed to see that Mrs. O'Ryan was in the right of it.

In the meantime, Lady Rosemary scrimped and saved and occupied herself with budgets and crops, gardens, and housekeeping, interests never meant for the daughter of a duke. "And it's not right," Mrs. O'Ryan had informed one of the skillets forcefully. "She never got to be a girl; she is no better than a servant in her own house. And never mind that she says she has no wish to marry. Who *could* she ever marry? There is no one suitable about to take an interest in her."

That lady would have been pleased to know that Lady Rosemary's own thoughts had taken a similar turn of late. She was not concerned for herself, however, for she still had her duties to perform. There would be time enough to determine her own future later. But she was beginning to worry about Isabella and Anne, both now of a marriageable age. She had no illusions about her father providing a season for them. That might come to pass should he think of it and have the money at the same time, but such a coincidence was highly unlikely, and the future of the girls could not be left to the fickle whims of fate and the Duke of Stedham.

Bella's illness last spring had frightened them all badly, and Rosemary was determined that her delicate sister would marry someone who would treat her kindly and give her an easier life. In fact, she heartily agreed with Mrs. O'Ryan, who had said when Bella grew ill, "How can she do otherwise, with her so sickly and living in this great, drafty barn of a house?" Bella must be cared for, and her silvery, ethereal loveliness and sweetness of temper made Rosemary believe that if only an eligible young man were available, he must surely love her.

And then there was Anne, a year younger

31

than Bella and as lively and quick-tongued as Bella was shy and soft-spoken. Her long, reddish gold hair was enough to stop any young man in his tracks, reflected Rosemary dolefully, if only there *were* any really suitable young men. She could not count Arthur Tipton or Richard Carter, for even though both came from perfectly acceptable families, everyone knew that they had to marry well. All that the Trevelyan daughters could offer was beauty. They had no fortune and their land was all entailed. Julian, of course, was a possibility for one of them, probably Anne—if his mother would ever leave him alone.

Rosemary knew that the girls' beauty had certainly begun to attract attention in the neighborhood, and her greatest fear had come to be that the girls would make unsuitable matches simply because there seemed to be nothing else for them to do. Bella especially must not be allowed to do so, for Rosemary knew that her fragile health would never withstand it. It did not seem likely that the daughter of a duke would make an unequal alliance, but then very few daughters of peers lived in their circumstances. There was a handsome young farmer or two, as well as an impoverished rector, who had come calling at Marston Hall far too often for her peace of mind. Rosemary was uncertain how she could make suitable matches for the girls, but she was quite determined to do so. If Papa would not provide them with an opportunity, then she would do so . . . somehow.

Rosemary did not pause to consider herself in this matter; indeed, as she had told Mrs. O'Ryan, she had no particular desire to marry, for she had quite enough on her plate at the moment without a husband to worry about. If an opportunity for an eligible marriage *had* presented itself, one that allowed her to care for her family, she would have married without question, but thus far there had been no such offer. She was not blind to her own dark-eyed beauty, and she knew she looked much like her handsome father, but she prized her beauty only as a possible means of rescuing the family. Buried in the country as they were and burdened with all of the household duties to perform, she had spent little time preening before a looking glass and dreaming of conquests. Her life had taken a more practical turn.

"Rosemary, dear," twittered a voice behind her, shaking her from her reverie. "Here is a letter from your dear father, just arrived from town." Miss Marian Trevelyan, followed closely by Miss Matilda, waved the letter at her.

"Thank you, Cousin Marian," she replied, taking the letter. It was most unlike her father to write, and she felt some misgivings as she took it to the small bookroom that served as her office and unfolded it. She read it not once, but several times, unwilling to believe its contents. Finally, she sat back and covered her eyes with her hands. "How *could* he be so foolish?" she murmured. She had never held a particularly high regard for his intelligence, but never had she known him to entertain such a crackbrained notion as this one.

A voice at the door caused her to glance up quickly, folding the letter and placing it to one side. Then, seeing who it was, she smiled in relief and held out her hands to the intruder. "Julian! You are just the person I needed to see. When did you return?"

"Last night, Rose," responded the dark-eyed young man in the doorway, taking her hands in both of his own. "I didn't expect such a warm welcome or I would have come earlier. I thought you might be angry with me."

"Well, I confess that I was not particularly pleased when you left in November without a word to any of us, but when I got your letter, I forgave you. After all, if your mother needed you, you had no choice but to go."

She did not add that she was quite sure that Mrs. Melrose had needed her son so desperately only because it had come to her ears that he was once again spending too much time at Marston Hall. Although their lands marched side by side and they had known each other from the cradle, Julian's mother had never been happy about their close relationship. As long as Julian's father had been alive, there had been no problem, for he had been fond of Lady Stedham and had encouraged the friendship between the two families after her death, feeling that that was the least that he could do for her children. After his own death two years ago, however, his good wife had done everything within her power to separate her son from the Trevelyan girls. Then, last summer, announcing that she had had her fill of country life, she had retired to Bath, and Julian had been left—at least for the moment—to manage their property alone. Things had gone smoothly for all of three months, and then she had sent for Julian, telling him that she was not well and that she needed his help with business affairs. Rosemary had been quite certain that she had something else in mind, and that her removal to Bath had been the first stage of a campaign to introduce him to other, more eligible, young ladies.

"And how is your mother's health?" inquired Rosemary, thinking to herself that Mrs. Melrose was doubtless enjoying her usual robust health.

Julian flushed a little and laughed. "Oh, Mother is well, of course—just in need of attention."

"And did she have a parade of young ladies for you to meet?"

He nodded sheepishly. "And one in particular, I'm afraid. I fear that I was a great disappointment to her when I was not in raptures over Miss Linden. She is a pleasant young woman, but she has no conversation and about as much liveliness as that desk. I did not think that I would ever be able to make my escape and return safely home."

Rosemary, who had a fair idea of Mrs. Melrose's idea of the perfect young woman, could picture the unfortunate Miss Linden quite accurately, and could not help laughing. "You know that you should not be speaking in such a manner, Julian. You are hopelessly rag-mannered."

He shrugged. "If I cannot say such things to you, Rose, then there is no one to whom I *can* say them."

And it was quite true. Despite Mrs. Melrose's fears, there was no idea of romance between the two of them, but they had been best friends since childhood, their relationship surviving even his years away at school. Had he been wealthy enough, Rosemary would not have been above setting her cap for him, but fortunately for him—and for their friendship—his fortune was a modest one, not adequate to the needs of Marston Hall and the Trevelyan family. Julian was older than she by only two years, and, being an only child, he had spent much of his time with the far livelier Trevelyan family. Until his death, Julian's father had advised Rosemary in the practical matters of running the estate, and Julian had done his best to step into the gap since then. Although Rosemary knew that there was nothing for

Mrs. Melrose to fear from their relationship, she had begun to wonder about Julian's feelings for Anne. However, he had said nothing, and she had never been one to pry. She did, however, hold the faint hope that something might come of this newborn interest.

At the moment, though, she had no thought to spare for Anne. She picked up the letter from her father and waved it at Julian, her eyes sparkling with indignation.

"You would not believe what my father has decided to do, Julian. I still cannot imagine that he would consider such an idea for a moment—he must have run mad. There can be no other explanation!"

She smoothed out the crumpled letter and read it again. "And I have no choice in the matter. By this time, it is already an accomplished fact."

He stared at her. "What are you talking about, Rose? Is he coming to Marston Hall? Is he remarrying? What is the difficulty?"

"I wish that he were marrying again—but I don't think such a possibility has ever crossed his mind. What he is doing is perfectly outrageous! Why—" She broke off as she crossed the room and closed the door firmly behind Julian, then waved him to a chair as faraway from the door as possible.

"I know that he does not mean for me to tell anyone, but I must!" Her voice was low despite her intensity.

"You know that you can trust me, Rose," he returned, taking her hand and patting it encouragingly. "Surely it can't be as bad as all that—" A sudden unwelcome thought crossed his mind. "Has he arranged a marriage for you?"

"Even if he were marrying me off to a man fifty years older than I, it would be preferable to what he *is* doing. He is arranging his own death, Julian!" Having stated it so baldly, she covered her face with her hands and began to laugh.

Julian looked at her in dismay, thinking that she was becoming hysterical, a state that was impossible to associate with Rosemary's usual composure. "What are you talking about, Rose?" he demanded, trying to keep his voice low. "Are you all right? Should I get Bella or Mrs. O'Ryan?"

Rosemary shook her head violently and made an effort to stifle the laughter that still rose treacherously in her throat. Taking the handkerchief that Julian offered, she wiped her eyes and sniffed loudly. "I'm sorry, Julian, but I just can't believe that he is doing such a thing! And you are the only one I can talk to about it. The girls mustn't know. At least not yet—not until I have time to think about what it is best to do."

"Then tell me, Rose," he said encouragingly, patting her hand again. "I've told you every crazy thing that my mother has done, so you needn't feel embarrassed."

"Believe me, Julian, what my father is doing at this very moment would make your mother look like the most sensible—and honorable—person in Christendom."

"What is it, then? I can't believe that he is really doing something to hurt himself or you couldn't sit here laughing about it."

Rosemary shook her head. "No, of course I couldn't. But what he *is* doing makes everything ever said about the Trevelyans true—that we are wild and irresponsible and half mad! It is no wonder that we have always been the subject of scandals. If this becomes known, we will be ruined!"

She paused a moment and stared at Julian a little wildly and then started to laugh again. "Of course—what am I talking about? We are already ruined. It is done. I had forgotten that—so I suppose it really doesn't matter."

Julian took her shoulders and looked her in the eye. "Rosemary Trevelyan, if you don't tell me the whole of this immediately, I will run into the hall and shout for the whole household to come in here."

He stood as though to carry out his threat, and she grabbed his coat sleeve. "No, no, Julian, you mustn't! It isn't a joke at all—I shouldn't have been laughing." She sighed and took a deep breath. "Sit back down, Julian, and I will tell you exactly what my father is doing."

Straightening her shoulders and wiping her eyes once more, she proceeded to explain. "He tells me in his letter that he is in desperate straits financially—which isn't an unusual condition for him—but apparently this is truly a disaster."

She stared blankly at Julian for a moment. "He says, Julian, that there is not even enough money to keep us at Marston Hall any longer. There is nothing left."

Julian could think of nothing comforting to say to this and so he simply patted her hand again.

"But he has had what he calls an inspiration. He is at sea right now, on a ship called the *Lovely Lady*—which is, of course, an appropriate name for a vessel he would choose," she added dryly. Her father's interests in a variety of women had been well known to Rosemary from her youngest days. This, in fact, was one reason that Lady Stedham had chosen to spend most of her time in the country with her children.

"At any rate," she continued, "he left a message for his man of business that he had received a message from a man to whom he had once lent a large sum of money—and that is believable, of course, for he is always lending money, whether he can afford it or not—and that this man could repay him the amount many times over if he would only meet him in Liverpool before he took ship for Canada. The captain of the *Lovely Lady* will report to Mr. Crispin that my father was lost at sea off the coast of Cornwall so that his heir will be notified immediately. Judging by the date," she said, looking down at the letter, "that has already been accomplished."

She smiled weakly at Julian, who was sitting with his mouth slightly ajar. "And so you have my father's plan for saving us from disaster."

"But, Rose, how in the name of heaven does that help anything?" Julian demanded, rising so abruptly from his chair that he almost knocked it over. He began to pace the length of the small room, rumpling his dark hair in aggravation. "So his heir—whoever he may be—comes and you are out of the Hall anyway. Your father has given his life for nothing!"

Before she could speak, he pulled her up from her chair, holding both of her hands and staring down at her earnestly, all laughter gone from his eyes now. "I will marry you, Rose, and your family can come to us at Melrose Manor. You and the girls and—"

"—and Merriweather and Uncle Webster and all of the children and Marian and Matilda," she added mischievously, her eyes beginning to dance. "Why there would be no problem at all. Your mother would be so very pleased, Julian. And of course it has been on the tip of

41

your tongue to offer for me for years! I wonder that you have waited so long to do so."

Julian, usually so merry, refused to rise to
the bait. "You know very well that I love you
and your family, Rose. I can't stand by and
see you put from your home."

Rosemary kissed him soundly on the cheek.
"And it was dear of you to offer, Julian. But
you may rest easily. My father, you will see,
has thought of everything. Sit down and listen
to the rest of the story."

Puzzled, he did as he was bid, and she continued. "You see, Julian, my father's heir is
young and unmarried, and he is quite convinced that when Aubrey Townsend—that's his
name—that when he arrives at Marston Hall
and spends a week or so, he must inevitably
fall in love with one of us, offer for her, marry
her in short order—I am to see to that—and
so save us all. And then, of course, my father
will miraculously reappear, having been saved
from a watery grave by some passing ship, his
wealthy new son-in-law will save us from ruin,
and we will all live happily ever after."

She sat back in her chair and folded her
hands. "Do you see any flaw in his plan, Julian?" she inquired innocently. Although she
had been distraught by the news herself, telling Julian had at least lessened the burden
and enabled her to see a certain humor in the
whole ridiculous situation.

Her friend sat staring at her. When he recovered, he shook his head slowly. "You are right, Rose. Lord Stedham has most certainly run mad. What an unforgivable situation to place you in!"

Talking to him had done her a world of good. Placing aside all thought of scandal—for they would have their fair share of that should they have to remove from the Hall because of her father's financial reverses—she began to believe that her father might be offering her the very opportunity she had been hoping for. She disagreed completely with his chicanery, although she had no choice but to go along with it, but he might be offering her the possibility of solving their problems.

"Not at all, Julian," she responded briskly, ignoring his look of astonishment. "I was thinking myself of how to provide proper marriages for the girls, for I knew Father would never think of it. And now, although it has been brought about by his own need, he *has* at least thought of it. If Aubrey Townsend is a presentable young man—and we know that he is a wealthy one—then it will be quite desirable for him to marry Anne or Bella."

She carefully averted her eyes as she mentioned Anne's name, for she felt quite certain that Julian had been drawn to her of late. To her way of thinking, it would be an ideal match, making her beloved Julian a member of the family at last and giving Anne a safe haven in this time of trouble. Nonetheless, she did not wish to press the matter, hoping that it would come about naturally now that Julian was back at Melrose Manor.

"And what if he wishes to marry you, Rose?" he inquired, his dark brows drawn closely together.

"I believe that I am too fond of giving orders for most young men to take kindly to—you have remarked upon that many times yourself, Julian—so that is not likely with Anne and Bella here, but I had already been thinking that I would marry the devil himself if he would but provide for my family," she responded calmly.

His dark brows snapped together as she spoke. "I don't like to hear you speak like that, Rosemary. You sound very cold and most unlike yourself."

"I must be practical, Julian. You know that." She stared thoughtfully at the empty fireplace and wrapped her shawl more firmly about her shoulders. Fires were a luxury allowed only in the living areas used by everyone. In the privacy of her office she merely bundled up a little more. "And it is fortunate that Father is such a stranger here. The girls will not be particularly distressed by his loss, for they scarcely know him."

"Rosemary!" He was shocked, even though he knew that she was right.

"Of course, I may tell them the truth about Father, but they will behave more naturally if

44

they do not know. And I can keep their thoughts from losing Marston Hall by telling them that there is no need to move directly," she continued ruthlessly, forcing herself to concentrate on the practical matters. "For I am sure that Mr. Townsend would not be so heartless as to ask us to remove immediately. I doubt he has any great interest in living here—the house in London will be a matter of greater interest to him, I am certain."

She paused and smiled gently at Julian. "Don't be upset with me, my friend. You know that we are indeed in desperate straits—and I know that I can turn to you if need be."

"You may be certain of that," he returned fiercely. "I would find a place for all of you. You must not think of pursuing such a course as you are speaking of, Rose. I would take care of all of you."

"I know that you would, my dear. But what I need most from you now is your laughter. If you can help me see the humor in this matter, I may be able to bring us through it successfully."

She patted his hand absently and turned to the window, watching the downy flakes of the first snowfall of the year settle across the wide stretch of lawn. "Now all we must do is wait for the announcement of Father's death and the arrival of Mr. Townsend."

Three

Their wait was a very brief one. Less than a week after their conversation a messenger arrived from Mr. Crispin, her father's man of business in London, bearing a black-bordered letter. Its pages informed Lady Rosemary Trevelyan and her family he had the regrettable duty of reporting to them that the Duke of Stedham had been lost at sea. He offered his condolences and, ever a practical man, assured Lady Rosemary that they need not worry about their circumstances for the time being. Since the new duke was a young, unmarried man, he would doubtless have little interest in settling himself at the Hall for some time to come. He asked also that they make no arrangements for their future without consulting him, promising that he would devote himself to looking after their interests.

As a matter of fact, he had already been doing just that. Crispin had been upset when the duke left London so abruptly, leaving him only a cursory note informing him that they would meet as soon as he returned from his journey, but he had been genuinely distressed when Captain Bing of the *Lovely Lady* had called upon him to report Stedham's death. Quite illogically, Crispin held himself at least partially responsible for the disaster, telling himself that had he shown more tact in telling the duke of his situation, he might not have rushed off on a fool's errand, taking ship with what was obviously a most unsavory character. For Captain Bing, a large, burly man who smelled strongly of rum, had inspired no confidence in Crispin. Had he seen any reason for doing so, he would have taken the captain before the authorities on suspicion of theft and perhaps murder, but when Bing appeared at Crispin's office to report the death, he had brought a portmanteau with the duke's effects. When requested to do so, Stedham's valet had sorrowfully inspected the contents of the bag and assured Crispin that everything was there, including the money that he had taken with him.

"There is not much, Mr. Crispin," said Baxter in a low voice, tenderly unpacking the bag. "His Grace did not have much of the ready, as you know."

Crispin nodded, guilt gathering round him like a dismal fog. "I wish that he had informed me of his plans, Baxter."

Baxter sighed lugubriously. "He left immediately after he received the note, Mr. Crispin. He would not even allow me to come along. If he had—well, if he had, perhaps he would be here now."

There was a brief silence while each of them considered what might have been. A sudden thought struck Mr. Crispin and he turned to the valet abruptly. "What of his emerald ring, Baxter?"

"He would never have removed it, Mr. Crispin. The only time he ever took it off was for me to clean it and then he put it back on immediately. The ring would have—gone with him."

"I see," sighed Mr. Crispin, reluctantly relinquishing the last of his suspicions of the captain.

Then Baxter added hesitantly, "Will you be writing to Lady Rosemary, sir? I'm afraid that this will come as quite a blow to the family. Do you know what will become of them now?"

This was a contingency that Mr. Crispin had not yet considered. The young ladies must, of course, be cared for. He once again straightened his narrow shoulders. "I will notify them of their father's death. And I will speak to Mr. Townsend about making arrangements for their care. He is not an unfeeling young man, and I am certain that he would not wish to see the young ladies left friendless."

He did not add that Mrs. Amelia Townsend was scarcely the soul of generosity, nor that she might not feel any such obligation to the Trevelyans. He would see to it that Mr. Aubrey Townsend behaved in a gentlemanly fashion toward his unfortunate relatives. He owed that much to the late duke.

And so it was that later that same afternoon Aubrey Townsend found himself facing a small, businesslike man across the desk in his comfortable library.

"My congratulations, Your Grace," said Mr. Crispin stiffly, finding the words oddly unfamiliar when applied to the fresh-faced young man before him.

"Thank you, Mr. Crispin," said the sixth Duke of Stedham gravely, looking down at the card that Crispin had sent in to him. "I am sorry to meet you under such circumstances. I'm certain that this has come as a great shock to everyone connected with the late duke."

Crispin nodded even more stiffly, but he was encouraged as he studied the young man's face. His blue eyes were intelligent, his bearing manly without appearing haughty, his expression amiable. Crispin decided to pay him the honor of speaking directly.

"I have come to you, Your Grace, not only to introduce myself and to offer my services, but also to appeal to you on behalf of the Trevelyan family."

Aubrey Townsend's eyes widened slightly at the mention of the family. Owing to the intervention of his mother, he had had virtually no contact with Trevelyan and had even less knowledge of his family circumstances. Indeed, he had felt little interest in the duke at all, feeling that it would be somewhat tasteless to press himself upon that gentleman's notice. Townsend was a very wealthy young man, and the acquisition of a title, although attractive to him, was not something that had kept him awake nights either. If he had given the duke's family any thought at all, it would have been to suppose that he had none. Certainly his mother had never mentioned them.

"In what way may I be of assistance to them, Mr. Crispin?"

"Aside from various distant relatives who are presently living at Marston Hall, there are also the four daughters of the late duke. I am sure that you can appreciate what a shock this will have been to them."

Townsend nodded and waited for him to continue.

"The young ladies range in age from thirteen to twenty-three, and at present there is no other place for them to retire to. I am certain that, given some time, I will be able to make adequate arrangements for them." He was certain of no such thing, but he must at least have a breathing space to consider the matter.

Townsend nodded pleasantly. Despite the fact that he was a singularly wealthy young man who had wanted for nothing, he was not a selfish person. "Of course they must remain at Marston Hall for as long as necessary, Mr. Crispin. I should not dream of putting them out of their home at such a time as this—nor do I have any immediate intention of taking up residence there. Take all the time that you need to arrange for their futures."

Crispin allowed himself a small smile of approval and coughed briefly. "There is also, Your Grace, the somewhat delicate matter of the upkeep of the estate while I am settling their father's affairs." Not in his wildest imaginings could he fathom how he would settle Stedham's affairs, but he would manage something.

Townsend waved his hand. "There is no problem. I am certain that my man of business can make the appropriate arrangements." He took a card from the desk and scribbled an address on it. "Here is his direction, Mr. Crispin. Please feel free to notify Devlin of the amount that is needed—and call upon him for any problems that may arise."

Crispin managed a genuine smile at this point. "You have been most kind, Your Grace. I am certain that the young ladies will be eager to express their gratitude to you themselves."

The door of the library had opened quietly, and a tall, gray-haired man entered the room and walked directly toward them. At first glance Crispin thought him a servant, but his manner seemed too self-assured. Townsend's kindly expression vanished when he saw the man, and it was clear that the intrusion was not a welcome one.

"I did not ask for you, Barron," he said briskly.

The gray-haired man smiled in a fatherly manner. "I know that you did not, Your Grace, but when I discovered that you had a caller who represented the interests of the late duke, I felt that you might have need of me."

"Thank you, Barron," returned Townsend in a voice that sounded anything but grateful. "I assure you there is no need. Mr. Crispin and I understand one another quite well. He will be calling upon Devlin and our solicitors to make all of the necessary arrangements—and he will, of course, feel free to see me if I may be of assistance to the late duke's family."

"Indeed," returned Barron disapprovingly. "I am certain that your dear mother, since she is herself indisposed, would wish for me to be present at any business meetings you might have."

Since being notified the day before of Trevelyan's unexpected death, Aubrey Townsend had been considering his own position carefully. He was an obedient son, but he was also a normal young man, and he had been growing more and more restive under his mother's restrictions. Frederick Barron, his tutor, was the most annoying one. Whenever he had attempted to free himself of this companion of his schooldays, reminding them that he was of an age to be entirely on his own, his mother, a fragile woman in poor health, had sighed and said she had always supposed it would come to this in the end, her only son disregarding her wishes.

On such occasions she would eye him wistfully from her invalid's couch and sigh. "I suppose that soon you will go away and leave me completely, Aubrey. And I suppose you *must* do so—it is the way of the world—to trample *roughshod* over the feelings of mothers."

Overcome by guilt at the sight of the tears she was obviously heroically repressing, he had given way upon every occasion. He was aware that, under the conditions of his father's will, he would come into his full fortune only when he married and established a separate household. That had once seemed no pressing matter, for he certainly had a more than adequate amount of money at his command and he had a very comfortable life. Nonetheless, since leaving Oxford he had begun to feel that an early marriage was absolutely necessary if he were to have any peace of mind. Surely a wife—any wife—would be easier to bear. His mother's tearful tyranny and her habit of speaking with dramatic emphasis had become too much to live with on a daily basis.

Her brother, Robert Avery, Earl of Barrisford, had informed her—and Aubrey—that such behavior was no better than emotional blackmail. "What would you have him do, Amelia?" he had demanded upon more than one occasion. "Do you want him to live his whole life at your beck and call? Are you ever going to allow him to become a man in his own right?"

Amelia Townsend had straightened her frail shoulders and glared at him. "You have *no* understanding of the matter, Robert! You have no child of your own, so you have *no* idea what it is to put another person's welfare before your own. You are what you have *always* been—first, last, and always—selfish to the core!"

"Well, I see that in that one thing we are alike, my dear sister," he had responded smoothly. "The difference is that I acknowledge my selfishness quite freely—while you disguise yours as a mother's love. I wonder when Aubrey will see it for what it is and kick over the traces."

He had strolled casually to the door as she lay fuming upon her couch. At the doorway, he had turned and smiled, firing one last shot before his departure. "I do hope that I am there to see it happen, my dear." And he had closed the door gently behind him before she could respond.

Barrisford had been urging Aubrey to take charge of his own affairs, but somehow he had seemed unable to do so. "That's all very well for you to say," he had informed his uncle, "but you don't have to live under the same roof as Mother."

"Nor do you," his uncle had pointed out. "You are a man of means, and you are of age. You need not marry in order to establish a separate household, merely in order to receive your full inheritance. Why should you remain in a situation you dislike?"

Aubrey had reflected that it was easy enough for his uncle to give that sort of advice, but he did not have to deal with the recriminations of a distraught parent for whom he still had a lingering affection. He had pointed that out, and Barrisford had agreed with him, noting that he had not realized until that moment how much he had to be thankful for.

Aubrey had given little thought to being next in line for a dukedom, for it seemed likely that Trevelyan, who was in excellent health, would live to a ripe old age. Now it seemed to him that, having unexpectedly become a peer of the realm, he had arrived at an appropriate moment to break the leading strings once and for all. He felt instinctively that if he did not seize this moment, he would remain forever under the control of Barron and his mother.

Accordingly, his tone grew sharp. "Barron, I would remind you that you are in my employ, not that of my mother. I realize that your years as my tutor have made you reluctant to recognize that I am of an age to handle my own affairs, and so I can—just this one last time—overlook your placing yourself in the midst of my private matters. I think that with my change of circumstance, your presence will be no longer required, although I will certainly provide you with an allowance so that you may have time now to pursue your scholastic interests."

Barron's pale face had grown even paler. His charge had periodically tried to free himself before, but never had Aubrey addressed him in such a tone.

"Very well, Your Grace. I must bow to your wishes, of course. However, I am doubtful that Mrs. Townsend will agree with this decision." Barron smiled faintly at the young man, obviously feeling that this reminder would bring him to his senses.

"It makes little difference whether she does or does not," answered her undutiful son, much to the tutor's amazement. "As I just pointed out to you, you are in my employ, not that of my mother. If she wishes to retain you to take care of her business affairs, she may certainly do so, but I assure you that there will be no more of your meddling in mine."

Crispin had withdrawn discreetly to a window and stood looking down on the street below, inwardly applauding the young man's actions. He had taken an instant dislike to Barron, and was pleased to see that Townsend appeared to be quite capable of handling his own affairs.

After Barron had bowed his way stiffly from the room, Townsend turned apologetically to his guest. "I am sorry that you were a witness to that, Mr. Crispin, but it seemed to me the moment to take care of the matter." He paused and then added boyishly, "I have waited for years to do just that."

"I am sure you have, my lord," returned Crispin affably. "It does not seem to me that young gentlemen ever wish to be kept on a leash."

"Well, I certainly do not, at any rate, and I have done with it." His forehead creased for a moment. "I was about to say something to you when Barron interrupted," he mused, and then he brightened as he remembered. "You were telling me of the Trevelyan ladies, Mr. Crispin. It seems to me that since I am the nearest male relative, it would be only right for me to journey to Marston Hall to assure them personally that they must consider it their home for as long as they have need of it—and to see if there is anything else I might do to help them. It would appear very odd if I were to neglect them at such a time. I will leave for Marston Hall as soon as possible." He did not add that he would be very grateful to have a reason for leaving London with all possible speed to escape his mother's reproaches, but Crispin, being familiar with the reputation of Mrs. Townsend, understood him perfectly.

Crispin bowed. "I am certain that they would be most grateful for your attention, Your Grace."

"With your permission, Your Grace, I will send a message to Lady Rosemary that you are coming so that they may be prepared."

Townsend nodded his thanks, already planning his escape from London. Not only would he leave behind Barron, but he would also refuse to take his elderly valet, who was another that regarded him as a child to be watched over. It was particularly fortunate, he thought heartlessly, that his mother had taken to her bed again. Surrounded as she was by her doctors and her companion and her maid, it would be some time before Barron could make his grievance known. He smiled to himself. This might even be the suitable time to take a wife and assume entire control of his fortune and his life.

Having settled matters to their mutual satisfaction, the two men parted company, unwittingly having set in motion the first steps of Jack Trevelyan's plan.

Rosemary had decided against sharing the news of the plan with her sisters, relying solely upon Julian for moral support. The family had received the news of Stedham's death reasonably calmly, although there had of course been some tears. The older ladies in particular had felt that a decent amount of distress was required to show their respect for the head of their family, their patron. Rosemary had minimized the grieving as much as possible, for, as she had told Julian, very few of them, even his own daughters, really knew the duke at all. And it was, of course, almost Christmas, and there were the children to consider.

When they received the news that his heir would soon be with them, their thoughts were given a new direction. Since Mr. Crispin had confided to Lady Rosemary in his message that the new duke wished for them to remain at Marston Hall for as long as they wished, she had shared that happy news with the others immediately and that had allayed some of their fears. All in all, they were prepared to regard the visit of the new duke as an interesting and cheerful break in their quiet lives, and Rosemary, of course, was determined to make the most of the diversion.

"What do you suppose he is like, Rose?" asked Bella dreamily, as they sat near the fire in the kitchen, the only warm room in the house. "Do you think he will be young and handsome?"

"You read too many romances," returned Candace practically. "He probably weighs too much and has spots."

Rosemary laughed, ignoring Bella's startled

expression. "Well, we know at least that he is young, Bella, and he seems to be kind, so those are points in his favor. We shall have to wait to see the rest." Inwardly, she hoped that he would be everything desirable in a young man. If her father's plan fell through because Aubrey Townsend was unattractive, they would all be without a home.

"What will he think of us for not being dressed all in black?" asked Cousin Merriweather a little plaintively, looking down at her dark blue gown. "That scarcely seems respectful."

"Mr. Crispin will have told him of our financial circumstances, so he will undoubtedly think that we have not enough money to provide all of the household with the proper mourning clothes," returned Rosemary briskly. "We are wearing our darkest gowns and we have trimmed them with black ribbons and purchased black gloves. The boys and Uncle Webster are making do with black armbands. I am sure that Mr. Townsend—the duke—will understand."

"Still," said Cousin Merriweather, her plump face showing lines of distress, "it does not seem quite respectful to the memory of the dear duke. And he was always such a proper, well dressed man."

"Proper" was scarcely a word that Rosemary would have considered applying to her father. Well dressed he most definitely was, however.

His family might have felt the pinch of financial strain, but Jack Trevelyan had never denied himself anything. He considered himself a generous man, sending presents to his family whenever he happened to remember he had one.

"Merriweather, you know very well that there have been no new clothes for anyone in the household since Father sent things a year ago," she returned a little impatiently. "I don't see how we could possibly afford even one mourning outfit for each one of us."

Recognizing the truth of this, Merriweather went meekly back to her mending, attempting to repair the shirt that Will had ripped when he had fallen from a tree earlier that afternoon. The sharp, bare branches had made a mess of both the shirt and Will. While Merriweather labored over the shirt, Anne labored over Will in the nether parts of the kitchen, ably assisted by Mrs. O'Ryan and Candace. His vigorous protests effectively masked the sounds of arrival at the front of the Hall, and so the ladies were taken by surprise when Matilda appeared in the doorway, accompanied by a stranger.

"Oh, Rosemary, my dear," she fluttered. "The duke is here. That is, the *new* duke is here."

She lowered her voice to what she obviously thought was a level inaudible to the gentleman standing just behind her. "It was too cold to leave him in the great hall. We could see our breath before us as we talked. I thought it would be better to bring him back here where he could warm himself."

To her annoyance, Rosemary found herself flushing. They had not expected Townsend until the next day, and she had intended to have fires lighted in the south drawing room and the library, as well as the apartment which he would occupy. She had every intention of showing her sisters to the greatest advantage. Instead, he had found them seated in the kitchen with the servants, wearing their oldest clothes.

This circumstance did not, however, seem to have disconcerted their guest at all. Townsend, a well-bred young man, remained behind Matilda for a moment and allowed his hostess time to regain her composure, for he had noted her rising color as she listened to his guide's whispered explanation. He had an excellent view of the scene before him, and, though it seemed extremely odd to find ladies seated in the kitchen, he could not help admiring the attractive picture that they made.

Having allowed Rosemary an adequate amount of time, he stepped forward and bowed to her, smiling. "Lady Rosemary, you must forgive me for intruding upon you unexpectedly. I was eager to arrive here so that I could place myself at your service during this difficult time. I hope that you will accept my

sincere condolences for your father's death—
and my apology for making you uncomfortable."

Rosemary found herself looking into such
friendly blue eyes that it was no effort at all
to smile at him and welcome him. She thought
to herself that Candace had been quite out
with her suppositions. Townsend was far from
fat and he certainly did not have spots. He
was a well-made young man and his hair and
skin were both the color of honey, having the
same dark golden smoothness. Her father's
plan might be easier to execute than she had
thought.

"Thank you for your concern, Your Grace—
and for your long journey in such cold
weather. I fear that we are not prepared to
receive you as we had planned, but I hope you
will come close to the fire here, and Mrs.
O'Ryan will bring you something hot to drink
while you thaw a bit. In the meantime, we will
prepare your chamber—and a more suitable
room for us to withdraw to."

"This fire looks delightful," he returned
cheerfully, moving briskly to the blazing hearth
and warming his hands there, acting as though
standing at a kitchen fire were one of his eve-
ryday activities. He gratefully accepted a
steaming mug from Anne, and was then introduced to the rest of the family.

After a very few minutes it was obvious to
Rosemary that he was winning the rest of the

group with his easy manner and his willingness to be pleased. She could hear Matilda making small chirping noises behind her and correctly interpreted them as her stamp of approval. Even Candace and Will appeared to regard him with some interest, for he stopped beside the puppies and patted them, talking knowledgeably of the terriers and their ability as ratters, and he inspected Will's newly acquired wounds with an admiring eye, listening to the circumstances of his fall with gratifying attention. Seeing the book in her lap, he talked to Bella of Sir Walter Scott and the Highlands, and with Uncle Webster he reminisced about a visit to the Isle of Skye. Only Anne stood a little to the side, watching him carefully—and a little suspiciously. But she, too, fell prey to his charm when he inquired if any of them enjoyed riding.

"It's Anne who is the bruising rider," announced Candace in a voice that brooked no opposition. "Julian says that she rides better than most of the men around here."

"Is that so?" asked Townsend, looking at her with interest. Anne's eyes had a dangerous sparkle, whether because of his look or the mention of Julian's name Rosemary was unsure. "I hope that you will ride out with me one morning, Lady Anne."

"She rides every morning," Candace informed him. "You only have to get up early enough and you could join her."

Seeing Anne's eyebrows arch at this casual arrangement of her business, Townsend hastened to say tactfully, "Perhaps after I have been here for a while, if she would not mind, Lady Anne could show me about the estate."

"Of course," returned Anne ungraciously. "I am sure that you must be anxious to see your inheritance."

Lady Rosemary frowned at her rudeness, but before she could smooth matters over, Cousin Merriweather, horrified by Anne's lapse of manners, had hurried into the breach.

"Well, of course, he would like to see all of it—I mean, it is, after all, only natural—anyone would want to see what—that is, I'm sure that he would enjoy a ride, Anne."

She gazed at her young cousin reproachfully, but Anne was impervious to such tactics. Plucking a woolen cape from a peg near the door, she announced abruptly, "I must go down to the stables now. Martin and I had put a poultice on Dover Boy's foreleg and I need to check it."

The door closed sharply behind her and, seeing her chance, Rosemary took the opportunity to smooth over Anne's rudeness. "She has been very worried about Dover Boy," she explained to Townsend. "He is her favorite, even though he is growing a little old." Rosemary was well aware that Anne had been distraught since her father's death, thinking that their horses would soon belong to his heir. She had spent most of her time since the announcement of his death in the stables.

"Very understandable," said Townsend, thinking to himself that this was quite the oddest household he had ever visited. He had never known of young ladies who sat in the kitchen amidst servants and dogs and who took care of their own horses. He thought ruefully for a moment of what his mother's reaction to this situation would be; then he recalled that he was alone and made himself as comfortable as possible on the settle next to the fire.

Watching the scene before him and visiting absently with Uncle Webster and the older ladies, Townsend found his eyes turning again and again to Lady Rosemary. She was, apparently, briskly organizing Candace and the children and their one maid to prepare his bedchamber and one of the drawing rooms. He admired her bright eyes and her graceful movements, but more than those, he took note of the kindly manner in which she spoke to the others. It required little imagination to understand how she must feel about having him arrive unexpectedly and find her in such a situation. Still, she maintained her cheerful composure, and, accordingly, those about her—with the possible exception of Lady Anne—reflected that attitude.

The only women he had ever known well were his mother and a young cousin slightly older than he. Certainly neither of them had Lady Rosemary's charming manner. Nor had any of the young women he had encountered while at Oxford or in the drawing rooms of London. Of course, he knew that, thanks to the stifling supervision of his mother and Barron, his experience had been extremely limited, but he was still quite certain that Lady Rosemary was a most unusual—and delightful—young woman.

On his journey to Marston Hall he had considered the matter of marriage and he had thought guiltily about Jack Trevelyan's daughters. After thinking over Crispin's words and what he had heard his mother say of the late duke, he knew that their situation could not be a happy one. For a moment he had considered the possibility of offering for one of them and so salving his conscience for displacing them. That had at first seemed farfetched to him, but now, having seen them—particularly Lady Rosemary—that possibility grew more attractive all the while.

He stretched his top boots toward the fire and sipped his hot ale in contentment. Never before had he felt quite so free. It was a delightful sensation, he decided. Never again would he allow others to control his life.

Four

The days that followed were, to Townsend's
way of thinking, idyllic. He had never been in
a household so cheerful and informal. He
abandoned the hours—and the airs—of a fash-
ionable young gentleman and arose early in
the morning with the others. He rode the
countryside with Anne, who treated him graciously as soon as she understood that the
horses were Trevelyan property and not a part
of his estate. He walked with Uncle Webster,
enjoying the old man's stories of the Highlands. He sat by the fire with Bella and the
elderly cousins as they sewed and chatted, telling him stories of the family; he played at
jackstraws and Charlie-over-the-water with Candace and the children.

These might have seemed very tame activities to a young gentleman accustomed to a
round of much more worldly activities, but he
found them strangely comforting. Not only was
he treated as a guest, but he was also accepted

as an adult. No one, of course, ordered him about or asked him to do things he did not wish to do. And he had made decisions on his own for the first time in his life.

It had become plain to him within his first hours at Marston Hall that they were indeed in straitened circumstances, and he had made arrangements in the village for Mrs. O'Ryan and Lady Rosemary to be able to order what they needed for the household. Accordingly, the meals had grown more interesting, new linens had appeared upon the beds, the children were wearing new clothes, and Bella had a new book to read by the fire.

Thus far, however, he had not been allowed to do anything for Lady Rosemary, and it was she, more than anyone, that he wished to serve. He found himself watching her whenever possible, admiring her graceful step, her kindly manner with everyone in the household, whether stablehand or lord. He had been amazed to find that there was no longer any bailiff, that her father had dismissed him two years ago, allowing Lady Rosemary to assume the majority of his duties. It appeared to him that she had more to look after than anyone should have, particularly a woman of gentle birth, but she went about her affairs with a cheerful air, never complaining.

For her part, Rosemary was very pleased with Aubrey Townsend. He was generous and eager to be pleased, quite different from the manner of young man she had expected. She had carefully encouraged his interest in Anne and Bella, watching with pleasure when he spent time with them. She could not detect a more decided interest in one than the other, however, unaware that his eyes followed her whenever she was in the room.

Whenever her conscience rose against her, telling her that they were taking unforgivable advantage of his good nature, she reminded herself sharply of the consequences if they did not. There would be no Marston Hall, no place to live for her and all of her brood. She had too many people who depended upon her to allow a tender conscience to stand in her way.

Accordingly, she arranged an informal at-home, anxious to give the girls an opportunity to dress up so that he could see them at their best. Despite the fact that they were officially in mourning, Rosemary disguised her small party as a get-together for a few of the county families to meet the new duke. She did not allow herself to think of what would happen when the *old* duke once again put in an appearance.

"After all," she explained to Cousin Merriweather, who had been dubious of the propriety of having such a social gathering so soon after the news of her father's death, "everyone is anxious to meet him, and it seems discourteous not to have them in to do so. And it

70

isn't as though there will be dancing, Merri-weather," she reminded her. "Just cards and games and conversation. And we don't wish to offend him by failing to pay him the proper attention."

Merriweather, who was anxious for a little merriment herself, allowed herself to be persuaded, and everyone prepared for the evening with pleasure.

Julian was the first to arrive that evening, greeting everyone with the assurance of one who is a member of the family. He had been a regular caller at Marston Hall for the past few days, both to offer Rosemary moral support and to keep an eye on Townsend. He considered it his duty to look after the Trevelyan girls, and he had been faithful in the execution of that duty.

Townsend felt an unaccustomed pang of jealousy as he watched Julian carelessly hug Lady Rosemary and plant a kiss on her cheek. She was, he had decided, everything that he could desire in a wife, and he had made up his mind to offer for her. He knew that it was just a matter of time before someone arrived from his mother—possibly his uncle. At least he hoped it would be his uncle. Barrisford, he felt, might be trusted to understand that he needed to marry in order to make the final break with his mother and gain control of his fortune. And surely he would understand when he looked at Lady Rosemary.

He made the rounds of the drawing room with her, meeting the Tiptons and the Carters and the Haverfords and Colonel Forester and Lord Burgston, who was seated by the fire with his gouty leg propped upon a stool. Having made polite conversation with all of them, Townsend finally managed to draw her to one side.

"Bella is looking particularly well tonight," he observed, wishing to say something that he knew would please her.

"Yes, she is," agreed Rosemary, her eyes warm upon her sister. "It was very good of you to buy those ribbons for her, and that shawl. The colors *look* wonderful on her. You have been very kind to us, my lord."

He smiled down at her, his eyes tender. "I hope that you will come to think of me as more than kind, Lady Rosemary." Then he surprised both of them by taking her hand and kissing it. He was quite certain that he could look for years and never find so agreeable a wife.

"Forgive me for saying so, Lady Rosemary, but I can see that you have not had the life that you deserve. I hope that I will be allowed to make that up to you."

She stared up at him in amazement. There was no mistaking the light in his warm brown eyes; she had seen it before with less eligible suitors.

"May I have the honor of making you my

wife?" he asked gently, oblivious to the interested gaze of some of the others in the room.

Rosemary took a deep breath. This was not what she had expected, but there was no reason to think it over. She had made her decision about any eligible offer of marriage for herself long ago. If the suitor could and would care for her family, she would accept him. Nonetheless, she hesitated for a moment, wondering at the suddenness of the proposal and thinking somewhat guiltily of his youth.

"This seems very hasty, my lord," she said gravely. "You have known me less than a day. Should you not wait a bit and think things over?"

He shook his head. "I have determined that I must marry, Lady Rosemary, and I have met no one who pleases me as you do."

Accordingly, she returned his steady gaze and attempted to sound as appreciative as she knew she should be. "Then I would be honored, Your Grace," she said softly, then lowered her lashes demurely, trying not to imagine what Julian and the others would say.

The die had been cast.

Robert Avery, Earl of Barrisford, having finally arrived at his home on Upper Grosvenor Square after seven months abroad, wanted nothing so much as to be left in peace for at least his first evening home. It was immediately clear to him that it was not to be, however. As one of the footmen carried in his luggage, his butler, who had hurried out to welcome him home as he stepped from the carriage, drew him discreetly to one side.

"I thought, my lord, that you would wish to know that Mrs. Townsend is waiting for you in the drawing room." He spoke in the funereal tone of one imparting the news of the death of a loved one.

"The devil she is!" Barrisford exclaimed impatiently. "I don't want to see her now, Graves. Send her home!"

"I did suggest, my lord, that it would be better if she called upon you tomorrow after you had time to recover from your journey, but she was very firm. She wishes to see you today." He coughed discreetly. "She has been waiting for three hours—and she said to tell you that she has no intention of leaving without seeing you."

There was a sharp rapping on the glass of a window above them, and they looked up to see Amelia Townsend beckoning imperiously to Barrisford.

He sighed. "Well, I suppose that since there's no help for it, I may as well see her so that I can get some rest. I wish that her husband were still alive so that she could worry him with all of her problems. Women are the very devil, Graves! You were wise never to marry."

"Yes, my lord," agreed his minion sympathetically. "So I have always felt."

"I suppose that I should be grateful that I have only one sister," said Barrisford, "and that she has only one child. I shudder to think what my existence would have been had she had more."

Another series of sharp raps forced his steps up the steps and into the entrance hall, where Graves took his greatcoat and hat.

"If she has not gone in half an hour, Graves, come in and announce that I have had an urgent message from—who *is* in town now, Graves?" he demanded abruptly.

"I'm sure that I don't know, my lord, but I shall find out."

"Yes, do that. And then pick the most important of the lot and say that I have an urgent message from him and that I must leave immediately."

Graves permitted himself a small smile. "I will do so with pleasure, Your Grace. Perhaps the Prince Regent is in residence."

"The very thing," agreed Barrisford, straightening his coat and turning to enter the drawing room.

The door flew open before he could, however, and a fragile figure in blue appeared. "Robert! I have been waiting *forever!* I *must* speak to you immediately!"

Before he could speak, she turned to Graves. "And *don't* allow Jennings to unpack his things, Graves. The earl will be leaving again *immediately*."

Barrisford's expression was normally forbidding, but at her words his face grew so dark that the footman carrying in his luggage immediately increased his speed so that he could remove himself to a safer quarter.

His sister, however, was too preoccupied by her own problems to give such an attitude serious consideration. "It is of *no* use to look like a thundercloud, Robert. This is an *emergency!* I have gotten up from my *sick*bed to beg you for help. You *must* save my dear boy from those dreadful, dreadful Trevelyans!

"What do the Trevelyans have to say to anything, Amelia?" he demanded abruptly, accompanying her into the drawing room and shutting the door, much to Graves's regret. "I suppose Jack Trevelyan has finally managed to borrow money from Aubrey."

"Oh, how I *wish* that were the problem! I would be devoutly grateful if this *only* concerned money!"

Since Amelia was notably tight-fisted and greatly inclined to regard Aubrey's money as her own, her brother could be forgiven for looking surprised by her statement. Knowing that she would tell him her news only when she was ready, he sat down impatiently.

No sooner had he settled in his chair, however, than she was upon him, clutching his arm and literally dragging him back to his feet. "You cannot sit down, Robert! You simply *cannot!* You must leave immediately and bring Aubrey back! There is not a moment to be lost!"

He stared down at her in amazement. Amelia was always peremptory in manner, but this attack surpassed anything that she had been guilty of thus far. Barrisford began to feel that she had run mad.

"Bring Aubrey back from where?" he demanded. "What are you rattling about, Amelia?"

"He is at Marston Hall, Robert!" she wailed. "Have you not heard? Jack Trevelyan was lost at sea and Aubrey is the new duke!"

"Is he indeed?" Barrisford responded. "My congratulations to both of you then. To be the mother of a duke must increase your consequence among your friends."

"How can you *say* such a thing to me, Robert? You know perfectly well that I never wanted him to have this title. I had *prayed* that Jack Trevelyan would live to be one hundred so that Aubrey would *never* have to sink his money into those hopeless estates."

She sat down abruptly, her face crumpling as she searched for her handkerchief. "And it is *just* as I predicted! Not only has he begun to throw money into that worthless estate, but now he writes to me that he is going to *marry* the oldest Trevelyan chit!"

Barrisford's eyebrows rose, his attention captured at last.

Amelia took a letter from her reticule and waved it in the air. "And he is going to marry her *immediately!* You *know* that he would normally never do something so foolish. It is all part of a—of a *plot!*"

"Nonsense," returned her brother, unimpressed. "How ever did Barron allow something like this to happen?"

"Aubrey refused to take Barron with him." Disbelief was clear in her tone. "In fact, Robert, he *dismissed* Barron and left for Marston Hall without doing more than leaving a *note* for me. He has clearly been *bewitched!*"

"If he dismissed Barron, he must have been in full possession of his faculties," said Barrisford brutally, ignoring her shocked expression. "He should have done so before this."

"Robert, he is just a *boy!* He cannot go wandering about the country alone, falling into the hands of fortune hunters like the *Trevelyans!* You know what that family is like!"

Although Barrisford would have argued with her about Aubrey being merely a boy and he was pleased to hear of Barron's dismissal, he could not deny that the thought of his marrying one of the Trevelyans was disconcerting— particularly marrying one out of hand like this, for he knew that Aubrey could have had no prior acquaintance with them. A brief bit of dalliance was one thing; marriage was quite another. Like his sister, he felt that this might indeed be a plot to acquire the Townsend fortune.

"And that is not *all* of it, Robert!" Amelia went on, satisfied that he was at last listening. She waved the letter at him again. "Aubrey writes that he has reason to believe that Jack Trevelyan's death was *not* an accident. He says—"

"What does he mean by that?" interrupted her brother.

"How could *I* possibly know, Robert? He merely tells me that, and then he goes on to write that he is to be gone from Marston Hall for a week while he checks into the matter, and that he hopes that I am quite well enough to be there when he returns so that I will be present for the *marriage*. How *could* he write in such an unfeeling fashion to his mother?" she demanded.

Before he could respond, however, she went rattling on. "And whatever could he mean about Stedham's death, Robert? *Could* he be speaking of murder? What *is* going on at Marston Hall? They must surely have *bewitched* my son."

Here her face crumpled again and she reached for her handkerchief. Barrisford looked at her in irritation. Had she been less high-handed with Aubrey, he would not have kicked over the traces and done something so corkbrained as this. There was no doubt in his mind, however, that he would have to scotch this plan. He was fond of the boy and he could not let him make a mistake that he would pay for the rest of his life merely because his mother had handled him in a witless manner.

"And so you see, Robert, that you *must* find out what is going on and save him from those wild Trevelyans!" ended his sister, looking at him imploringly.

Barrisford walked to the door and yanked it open. His butler was lingering in the entryway, preparing to enter with the message that the Prince Regent required the immediate presence of the Earl of Barrisford.

"Graves, tell Jennings that I will be leaving immediately for the country. And have Hacker put to my curricle and the grays."

Graves looked shocked. It was seldom that his master was outflanked by Mrs. Townsend, and it grieved him to see it happen.

"How long should I tell Jennings you will be staying, my lord?" he inquired.

Barrisford smiled briefly—not a pleasant smile at all, Graves noted. "I will make very short work of this, Graves. Tell him that it is two days' hard driving from here, but I will not be remaining long. I have a small matter to attend to."

Five

The engagement of Rosemary and Aubrey
had been announced, and everyone—with the
exception, of course, of Julian—was pleased.
Not only would there soon be a wedding to
celebrate on New Year's Day, but there was also
Christmas fast approaching. Even though there
was much to be done, Mrs. O'Ryan could
scarcely contain her joy. Lady Rosemary was to
be properly married to a gentleman who was
worthy of her, and the new duke had told her
to order whatever she needed, both for the
kitchen and for whatever minor refurbishing
of the household that could be accomplished
in such a short time. To crown it all, she had
extra help from the village to turn the manor
inside out and scour it from top to bottom.

Rosemary had managed to tone down her
zeal a trifle, reminding her that it was impossible to do more than the living area they now
occupied, as well as two guest chambers to be
prepared for Aubrey's mother and uncle. To

undertake the cleaning of the rest of the manor, closed these many years, would be far too great an undertaking in so brief a time.

"But you will be able to do so soon, Mrs. O'Ryan," Rosemary had comforted her. "I know that you long to put the whole place to rights, and so you shall—but we haven't long now before we might have guests."

"He *is* a very fine young man, isn't he, Lady Rosemary?" asked Mrs. O'Ryan, her face shining as she prepared gingerbread for the children.

"He is indeed," agreed Rosemary, and wished that she could feel happier herself about the marriage. She was aware that she could scarcely have been more fortunate. Aubrey Townsend had shown himself to be kindhearted and generous to a fault. It had taken him very little time to take stock of their situation. His questions had been most delicate, but it was clear to her that he was horrified by their situation, and he had immediately set about trying to improve things. Mrs. O'Ryan was to have carte blanche at the shops in the village, ordering whatever supplies she needed; a dressmaker and her assistant were called in from the village to prepare new gowns for the ladies; Uncle Webster and the boys were sent shopping in the village for their new apparel.

Rosemary had tried to protest, but Aubrey had placed his finger over her lips. "You have tried to do everything yourself for too long a time, my dear. Now you must let me help you. After all," he added teasingly, "I am the new head of the household as well as your husband-to-be."

Her conscience, troubling her all the more because of his generosity, stabbed her. "But, Aubrey, this is too much for you to be spending. I'm sure that you have—"

He stopped her before she could finish. "You forget, Rose, that I am well-to-do, and that what I have is yours. You need not worry about your finances any longer."

His feeling of competence was an unfamiliar one for him, for he had never before had an opportunity to be in charge of solving a problem, but he was certain that he could at least improve the straitened circumstances of Rosemary's family. The feeling of accomplishment made him regard her even more affectionately. She had provided him with the opportunity to prove himself a capable manager, someone with no need of Barron or his mother. He thought with satisfaction of the horror with which they both would regard his actions.

Rosemary glanced at his handsome face and reminded herself once more that she was indeed a most fortunate young woman. Aubrey was protective and eager to please her. He had taken an interest in her family and in the estate as well. He had asked Anne to take him out riding to look over the property, and Anne had done so, spending several hours taking him to meet every tenant farmer on the place. She was more willing to ride out with him now that he was engaged to Rosemary—and showing no interest in taking over the horses. When they had returned, he had begun making plans to restore some of the tumbledown cottages he had visited, to drain an unhealthy bit of swamp that they had encountered, to plant fields that were presently lying fallow.

Rosemary was surprised by the twinge of jealousy she felt when he began to talk in such a manner, and the feeling grew even stronger when he informed her that he was going to have his man of business engage a bailiff to take charge of the estate.

"A bailiff!" she had cried. Then, seeing his surprise at her tone of voice, had tried to modify it. "But of course," she added hurriedly, "I know that you would not have time yourself to attend to affairs here." She had been thinking no such thing; she could only see her life as she had known it slipping out of her control and into the hands of another.

Aubrey had smiled then, thinking that he understood her, and she had wondered what he would think of her when her father appeared, safe and sound and ready to resume his rightful place as duke. It would naturally be all to the good so far as Trevelyan was concerned if Aubrey did take over the running of the estate at this point. Whether Aubrey would want to do so or not would be another question. What he would think of them if the truth came out about her father's "death" was still another question that she preferred not to dwell upon. At least, she comforted herself, he was very amenable to doing something for her sisters. He had, in fact, mentioned it on his own, saying that Anne would be a hit in London and that Bella must visit his mother's Harley Street doctor so that they could look after her fragile health. Candace was to have a governess, although she had announced that she preferred to have her lessons with Uncle Webster and her cousins.

Altogether, Rosemary reflected, since she must make a marriage of convenience, it could scarcely have worked out more to her advantage. Still, life seemed curiously flat now that she no longer had to worry how everyone would be cared for. Aubrey had assured her that they would live their lives in any manner that she wished. They could travel, which she had longed to do; they could live in London, which she had never seen; they could live at the Hall, which she loved; they could do all three. Before they were able to develop this agreeable topic in more detail, however, a letter arrived for Aubrey, and he had hurriedly packed a bag and announced that he had to make a trip to Liverpool but that he would be back within the week.

Rosemary was somewhat troubled by this, for

that had been the destination of the *Lovely Lady*. Still, she could not imagine that there was any connection and Aubrey did not seem inclined to discuss his business with her. Instead, he had kissed her, told the rest of the household goodbye, and left within the hour, reminding her to be on the lookout for his uncle, whom he also expected for the wedding.

"And so I shall be," she thought to herself dismally. She felt quite sure that his mother and uncle were not going to look with favor upon their sudden betrothal, and she ardently hoped that Aubrey would return before either of them arrived. He had not said a great deal about his mother, but his picture of his uncle had been glowing. Obviously the two were close, and Rosemary was quite clever enough to read between the lines. The picture of the Earl of Barrisford that she had pieced together from Aubrey's stories was that of an imperious, worldly man, difficult to please and not terribly fond of women.

She was, of course, quite accurate in her estimate.

To say that the earl was unhappy about his flying trip north would have been understating the case. He was weary after his long journey home; he had wished to see his friends and had engaged to spend the Christmas holidays in Kent; he was annoyed with his sister for her mishandling of Aubrey; he was irritated with Aubrey for being such a cawker as to be taken in by what he assumed must be merely another pretty face; he was angry with Lady Rosemary Trevelyan, who must, he had decided, have been cut from the same piece of cloth as her father. "A pretty piece of work it would be," he thought in annoyance, "if Aubrey has no more wit than to marry someone who has an eye on spending all of his money."

And just as he had thought that his journey could not be more tiresome, it began to snow. The cold had been piercing during this second day of his journey, almost forcing him to relinquish his curricle had he been willing to slow his pace, and the innkeeper where he had stayed the night had informed him that it had been freezing weather for the past week. Beyond a doubt, then, the snow would stick. How delightful it would be to find himself snowed in for the Christmas holidays with Aubrey's greedy in-laws-to-be.

He had stopped briefly at what he assumed would be the last posting inn on the main road to change horses and had kept them moving at a brisk pace for the next two hours, taking advantage of the waning hours of daylight. He paused in Tareyton, the nearest village, for directions to Marston Hall, and drove through the gates just as the evening dusk was beginning to thicken. It was still snowing lightly, and as he slowed his pace to make his way down the drive, barely discernible under the gathering snow. He could not yet see the Hall, but he could hear the sound of voices—a good many voices, it seemed to him. They seemed to be coming from the far side of a low hill that sloped down to the drive.

He stopped a moment and listened; then, curiosity overcoming him, he climbed from the curricle and made his way to the top of the rise, ignoring the damage he was doing to the gloss of his top boots. At the crest of the hill he paused. Below him lay a small lake, bending out of sight around a neck of land covered with snow-clad trees. The far side of the lake was also edged with trees. In the distance stood Marston Hall, smoke curling from several chimneys and its windows golden in the dusk.

On the frozen surface of the lake were what seemed to Barrisford countless children, several of them presently employed in playing a vigorous game of crack-the-whip. He watched as the "whip" cracked and the one on the end was sent spinning face-first and shrieking into a bank of snow below him while the rest of the group snaked back across the ice.

Grinning, he made his way down the hill to help the victim to her feet; she had collapsed in a heap and was shaking her head and trying to brush snow from her face with hopelessly snow-crusted gloves. Catching hold of her by the waist, Barrisford picked her up and stood her upright on her skates on the ice. Startled, she looked up at her rescuer, the hood of her dark cape slipping back.

She was no more startled than he. Because of her height, Barrisford had expected a chit of a schoolgirl; but he had realized as he held her that she was older than he had thought. Now, seeing her tumbled curls and scarlet cheeks, he realized that she was far lovelier than he had realized, too.

"That was very gallant of you, sir," Rosemary said, smiling and attempting to dust the snow from her cape. "Do you wander about the countryside looking for maidens in distress to rescue?"

He bowed. "I believe, ma'am, that you are thinking of Sir Galahad. I assure you, I am not he."

She laughed. "I am relieved to hear it. I always thought that must be a tremendously boring life. I didn't think much of the maiden's part in it either—always waiting to be rescued. It always seemed to me that they should be doing something to save themselves."

"My thought exactly," he responded, smiling down at her, admiring the contrast of her snow-frosted lashes and dark eyes. "I hope that I am forgiven for attempting to rescue you—I realize that you would have taken care of it yourself, of course."

"Eventually. Of course, if they had not chosen to release me here on the roughest part of the lake, I could have done it a bit more easily. The ice is smoother over there."

Barrisford could see that they were about to be descended upon by the rest of the skaters. Even the smallest one, pulling a box that appeared to contain a doll, was heading in their direction.

"I believe that you are about to be rescued from your rescuer, ma'am," he said, bowing over her small, snow-crusted glove. "May I be permitted to make myself known to you? I am Robert Avery—"

"You are Aubrey's uncle, Lord Barrisford!" she exclaimed. Fortunately, her cheeks were already scarlet with the cold so he could not tell that they had suddenly grown hot. She had certainly not planned to meet this man in such a manner.

He looked at her in amusement. "Yes, I am indeed Aubrey's uncle—"

Before he could continue, Will and Jamie, who had gotten close enough to hear, turned to relay the information to the others. "It's Aubrey's uncle, Lord Barrisford!" they shouted. "Come on, Rose, let's take him to the Hall so that we can all get warm!"

"I see that I was expected," he observed dryly. "And I take it that you must be Lady Rosemary."

She nodded. "Did you receive Aubrey's letter inviting you to our wedding?"

"No, I did not. I must have left before it arrived. I came—at his mother's request," he replied delicately, omitting the nature of her request.

"Will Mrs. Townsend not be coming herself?" inquired Rosemary, feeling a rush of hope.

"No, her—her health does not permit her to travel such a distance," he responded. "I am the family representative."

"Well, it was very kind of you to come, Lord Barrisford, particularly in weather such as this." She looked about for a moment. "Where is your carriage? Have you already been to the Hall or have you just come up from the drive?"

"My curricle is in the drive. I left my unfortunate horses tethered to the branch of a tree when I heard the shouting."

"Julian!" she called, beckoning to a tall young man who had remained a little at a distance. Would you get Lord Barrisford's curricle for him, please, while we take him up to the Hall to thaw?"

He nodded shortly, not approaching for an introduction but sitting down swiftly on a rock to unstrap his skates. The others were busily divesting themselves of theirs, and Barrisford surprised himself by kneeling beside Rosemary to unstrap hers.

"Just brace yourself on my shoulder, Lady Rosemary, and I'll have these off in a trice," he said briskly. To himself he was wondering what the devil he had fallen into.

As he watched the others racing up the hill, skates hung over their shoulders, he remarked casually, "I see that you are having something of a party today."

She looked at him in surprise. "Oh no, but it is the first day the ice has been solid enough for the children to skate on, so of course nothing would satisfy them but being out for the whole afternoon."

"They all live here?" he asked, his eyebrows high as he tried to remember how many he had seen.

"Yes—well, all save Julian, of course. He is a neighbor."

Thinking of Julian's barely repressed scowl as he had knelt to unfasten Lady Rosemary's skates, he thought to himself that he might be rather more than a neighbor, but he said nothing.

"They are all your brothers and sisters, then?"

"Oh, no, some are, of course—two of them, to be exact, for Bella is not well enough to be out and skating. The others are cousins."

"I see," said Barrisford as they started together toward the Hall, thinking to himself that he did not see at all. He had been trying to remember what he knew of Jack Trevelyan's family, and had decided that he knew virtually nothing.

"Aubrey will be delighted that you have come," said Rosemary pleasantly. "You are quite his hero, you know."

"I should hope not," he returned dryly. "I believe you and I have already discussed what we think of heroes. Is Aubrey not back from Liverpool then?"

She shook her head, and he noticed that a wrinkle appeared on the bridge of her small nose when she was puzzled. "I'm not sure when he will return because I'm not at all certain why he went. He received a note and said that he would back within a week. It has been five days now."

Barrisford wondered what on earth could have possessed his nephew to gallop off to Liverpool, of all places on earth. So far as he knew, Aubrey had never been there in his life. Nor had he ever traveled alone before. He grinned to himself. Well, at least he was doing something beyond the clutches of his mother and Barron—and Lady Rosemary Trevelyan. She was certainly not what he had pictured, but he had no illusions about her. She was surely a fortune hunter.

Six

Barrisford was not a man easily surprised or easily impressed, but his first day at Marston Hall was an occasion totally outside of his experience. Like his nephew upon his arrival, he soon found himself settled by the fireside with a cup of steaming punch. This time, however, thanks to the efforts of Aubrey and Rosemary, the guest was seated in the south drawing room. He was served, not by a butler, but by Lady Rosemary herself and a young maid who seemed terrified of him and more accustomed to the precincts of the kitchen than the drawing room.

He had attempted to count the children as they were trooping into the house, but they were too much in motion, and he had given it up as a lost cause. Now he seemed to be beset by small elderly women, for Cousins Merriweather, Miranda, and Marian all appeared in the wake of Lady Rosemary to be introduced to "dear Aubrey's uncle." They tactfully withdrew after their profusion of welcoming comments and Barrisford drew a deep breath and stretched out his long legs toward the fire. Then, just as he was settling back to relax, Uncle Webster appeared quietly in the doorway to bid him a good evening and to offer to bring him something to read.

Barrisford refused his offer pleasantly enough, feeling that he needed the time to sort through his impressions and, perhaps, to close his eyes for a moment while he waited for the fire just lighted in his chamber to remove the chill. Uncle Webster nodded understandingly and tiptoed away, again leaving their guest momentarily in solitary splendor.

As the old man silently shut the door behind him, Barrisford shook his head in disbelief. Who *were* all of these people? It appeared to him that Marston Hall had been turned into a sort of combination inn and orphanage. He knew that Jack Trevelyan had seldom spent time at Marston Hall, and he began to understand why. There probably wasn't a room left for him, he thought to himself. And if there had been, he would probably have gone mad in the midst of this hive of humanity.

Dinner that evening did nothing to correct his first impression. The children, he saw gratefully, had apparently been served earlier and had retired to the nether parts of the house, so the meal was more peaceful than it might have been. There were still, however, all of the elderly cousins and Uncle Webster and the young Trevelyan daughters. He managed to sort them out as they chattered, the older ladies eagerly sharing with him their impressions of "dear Aubrey." It was obvious to him that his nephew had been an unqualified success in the household. And why not, he asked himself cynically. He had apparently been very openhanded with his money and few things were more likely to win the approbation of the general public.

The Trevelyan daughters were pleasant, but less chatty. He decided as he looked at the three of them—for Candace was upstairs with the other children—that Stedham had been a fool for not bringing them to London. Barrisford was a connoisseur of accredited beauties, and the three at the table with him would have put many of those ladies to shame. The interesting thing, he reflected, was that they were none of them just in the common style nor did they resemble one another. Even the youngest one, Lady Candace, still in the schoolroom, had a particular look of her own.

Lady Anne's beauty was very vivid—making him think of the glow of flickering firelight—while Lady Isabella's was a silvery radiance, belonging to gentle moonlit nights. But it was Lady Rosemary who received his greatest attention. It was no wonder, he reflected, that his nephew had fallen victim to her charms. Many an experienced London rake would have done the same, for her loveliness was exquisite—a wealth of dark hair and a complexion that made him think of snowdrops. And yet it was not merely her prettiness that was captivating; her charm lay in the lively warmth of her eyes and the tenderness of her smile.

Despite himself, he found his gaze returning to her again and again—because of Aubrey he told himself sternly. He himself was far too old and wise to be taken in by a pretty face. That had happened only once in his life, and he had no intention of ever allowing it to happen again.

For a moment he allowed himself to remember, just as a reminder of what havoc a beautiful woman could wreak. It had been years ago when he had become engaged to a young woman generally considered to be the toast of London that season. Maria had been graceful, lovely, amusing—and completely false. Barrisford knew that he had been considered an extremely good match; cynicism told him it was his money more than his charm that made the difference. Maria, however, had made him believe that it was he himself who had won her, that his fortune and his title were nothing to her. Then she had discovered someone else who had as great a fortune and who was a marquis as well, and she had left him without a second thought, saying in her charming manner that she knew he would understand.

And he had, all too well. She had confirmed his worst suspicions about women.

Since then, matchmaking mamas had angled for him in vain. He was charming when he chose to be, but never to the same young woman more than once. His name had been connected with one or two dashing young matrons, but more often he was seen in the company of graceful and witty Cyprians. "There is no pretense with them," he had explained to Aubrey, ignoring the horrified protests of Amelia. "They are interested in me because I am a wealthy man. There is something very refreshing about honesty."

As he studied Lady Rosemary's lovely face, he reminded himself of Maria, and of the purpose that had brought him here to Marston Hall. Still, as he watched her talking with the others, he saw that her interest in the others seemed sincere. She did not speak to call attention to herself, but to draw out the others. Her manner was playful, but not coy. And the brightness of her eyes, he decided, was at least partially attributable to intelligence. He reflected that it might be more difficult to disengage Aubrey than he had at first thought.

When the cloth was removed, the ladies withdrew and left Uncle Webster and Barrisford to themselves. The little maid who had served their dinner brought in a decanter of port and two glasses, then left them in solitude. Uncle Webster declined the port, but took out his pipe and made himself comfortable, and Barrisford, filling his glass thoughtfully, decided that this would be a good time to acquire a little background information.

"And so you are Lady Rosemary's uncle, Mr. MacLean?" he inquired.

Uncle Webster nodded. "At least that is what they call me," he amended. "I am actually a second cousin of the late Lord Stedham, but it is easier for the young ladies and the children to call me uncle because of my age."

"I see. And you have lived at Marston Hall for a long while?"

Uncle Webster nodded again, studying his pipe earnestly. "I came three years ago for a visit, and Lady Rosemary asked me to stay to teach the children."

He paused, and then spoke again. "I knew, of course, that she asked me to do so because she understood that I had nowhere to go. I had owned a small place in the Highlands that had belonged to my parents, but I lost it after they died." He looked at Barrisford apologetically. "I am a scholar, you see. I was never bred to live on the land, and so when I lost it, I came here. I knew that Marston Hall was a grand place, and I hoped that I might be able to do some work for Lord Stedham in the library, or do some letters for him."

"And were you able to do so?"

Uncle Webster nodded. "Not really for Lord Stedham, though I know that is how Rosemary wished me to think of it. She is the one that set me to work and kept me busy for weeks. By the time I had accomplished the cataloging, Mrs. Halleck had died, and Rosemary told me that I would be doing her a great favor if I would stay and teach the children."

"And Mrs. Halleck was . . . ?"

"The sister of the late Lady Stedham. She came to stay here with her children after the death of her husband."

"And was Lady Stedham still living at the time?" inquired Barrisford curiously.

"No, she has been dead for some ten years. Rosemary has been in charge of the household for almost all of that time."

Barrisford looked at him in disbelief. "What age is Lady Rosemary? She doesn't look old enough to have been running a household for so long a time as that."

Uncle Webster chuckled and settled himself more comfortably with his pipe. "She wasn't old enough to take it on, but she did it anyway because there was no one else. You can see for yourself that Merriweather couldn't say boo to a goose, let alone take care of a gaggle of children and an estate."

Barrisford sipped his port reflectively. There was more to Lady Rosemary than he had at first suspected. Not that it made any real difference, of course. It was no wonder that she was eager to marry and to be free of some of her responsibilities. Nonetheless, he would have to watch her. This merely meant that she was more dangerous than he had thought.

Pleading weariness after his journey, he excused himself soon after joining the ladies in the drawing room. On his way to his chamber, he tripped over a small morsel of humanity huddled on the stairs. Holding his candle closer to the floor, he inspected the child.

"You are Charlotte, aren't you?" he inquired.

She merely nodded mutely, clutching her small wax doll closer to her.

"Are you feeling quite well?" he asked helplessly, wishing that the child would take herself away to wherever she had come from. With the exception of Aubrey, children had been quite outside of his experience and he had every intention of keeping things just that way. Still, it seemed heartless to ignore her.

She nodded again.

Barrisford was eager to get to his chamber, but he was reluctant to abandon her to the dark and cold of the stairway. "Do you need something? Could I help you?"

She nodded emphatically and stood up, taking his free hand as she did so. "Want Rose," she replied simply, and waited confidingly for him to lead her downstairs.

Turning, they made their way carefully to the bottom and along the passageway to the drawing room, her small sticky hand tucked safely into his.

"Excuse me," he said, reentering the room with Charlotte in tow. "There appears to be an urgent need for you, Lady Rosemary."

"Charlotte!" she exclaimed, coming over to scoop her up. "I thought you were asleep."

The morsel shook her head and rubbed her eyes. "Want puppies!" she announced emphatically. "Want them *now!*"

"Do you indeed?" asked Rosemary cheerfully, heading for the door. "Let's go along and see them then. It's too chilly for you to be wandering about, Charlotte. You'll catch cold and then you'll miss going out to gather the greens for Christmas."

Charlotte's eyes grew wide at the thought of missing this treat, and she burrowed into Rosemary's shoulder. Barrisford noted that her small mouth was scarlet, decorated with what appeared to be raspberry jam, doubtless the source of the stickiness he had been so keenly aware of. Taking out a handkerchief, he followed them to wipe away the offending jam before Charlotte smeared it across the shoulder of Rosemary's green gown. Then, to his own surprise, he took Charlotte into his arms.

Lady Rosemary stared at him in surprise. "Why, thank you, Lord Barrisford—but there is no need for you to carry Charlotte. She will entirely disarrange your clothing." She watched in some distress as Charlotte continued to burrow, doing significant damage to his intricately knotted and once snowy neckcloth.

Barrisford gritted his teeth and wondered what had possessed him, but he managed a brief smile. "It is no trouble, Lady Rosemary. It was difficult for a moment to discern which of you was carrying the other." And that was quite true, for Charlotte was quite tall for a three-year-old, and Lady Rosemary, although well-formed, was short, which had led him to his mistaken identification of her as a school-girl earlier at the lake.

Smilingly accepting his words, she led him to the kitchen, where they found Mrs. O'Ryan, Candace, and Robert comfortably established by the fire. The two children were each feed-ing a pup, and Barrisford and Lady Rosemary seated themselves on the settle, Charlotte nes-tling comfortably in Barrisford's arms while they watched. Mrs. O'Ryan supplied her with a mug of warm milk and Rosemary watched fearfully while she sipped it, picturing a sud-den cataract of milk flowing across the earl's flawlessly tailored black jacket.

To her relief, no such disaster occurred, and, since Charlotte soon began to nod, thanks to the warmth of the milk, the fire, and Bar-risford's arms, she was soon able to guide them upstairs to the nursery. Barrisford re-fused to relinquish his charge, saying briskly that he had no desire to feel guilty because Lady Rosemary had broken her neck on the stairs while attempting to carry a child half her own size.

Once Charlotte was safely in the nursery, Rosemary adjusted the fender and screen in front of the fire and rearranged the covers of her bed so that Barrisford could put her down. As he did so, Charlotte blinked sleepily and artlessly completed the ruin of his neckcloth by hugging him and removing the last traces of milk from her lips.

When he was safely within the protective walls of his own chamber, he wondered what had possessed him. He was not fond of children, and he had found himself in a veritable infant hothouse; he disliked the company of dithery old maids, and he was surrounded by them; he detested young women who were shopping for husbands, and he had stumbled into a covey of them. Amelia and Aubrey had much to answer for, he reflected darkly. He would straighten this matter out as soon as Aubrey returned, and, if good fortune were his, they would be back in London by Christmas Day.

Seven

The next morning he strolled into the dining room at what he considered an unreasonably early hour, only to discover that everyone else had apparently not only risen and dined, but had also repaired to some remote region of the Hall—a situation which suited him down to the tassels on his polished Hessians. He took a slice of toast from the rack and settled himself comfortably close to one of the windows overlooking the lake, admiring the softness of the landscape after the gentle snowfall of the night before.

The swath of snow between the windows and the lake was perfectly smooth, perfectly white, and he allowed himself to sink into a reverie as he stared at the sunlight glinting against its surface. At least he had not been snowed in with the Trevelyans, and Aubrey should be able to make the drive from Liverpool with relatively little trouble.

Perhaps it had been a mistake to come

home to England. At least while he was traveling his time was his own; Amelia had not yet tried to keep up with him once he got outside the country. He smiled. There was much to be said for Europe. He had had Aubrey's company for two months in Italy and had enjoyed it profoundly, but then they had parted company and he had wandered on to the Greek Isles alone. He was never lonely; he made friends when he pleased to make them, but he was happy in his own company, too. When he tired of a place—or of the people there—he simply left.

His peaceful reverie was rudely interrupted when Robert and Will suddenly raced into view, pursued by the other children, and a noisy game of hunt the fox ensued. Soon they were joined by Lady Rosemary and her sisters, all wrapped in capes and bearing baskets, walking in the direction of the woods. Even Charlotte was there, a hat pulled firmly over her curls. She was stalwartly trudging through the snow at the moment, but Barrisford wondered how long that would last. Soon someone would be weighted down by her as Lady Rosemary had been last night.

They were most certainly going to gather greens to decorate the Hall, snow or no snow. He watched as they trooped off toward the distant woods and smiled as he saw Charlotte suddenly stop and hold up her arms. To Lady Rosemary, no doubt.

He stared down at his boots ruefully for a moment, then rose and walked briskly to his room. Pulling out the pair that he had ruined in the snow last night, he quickly put them on and hurried downstairs. They were just disappearing into the woods as he left the Hall.

Amelia should see me now, he thought, chuckling to himself. She would be certain that he had at last run mad. She had thought it coming any time these past ten years. And perhaps she had a point. After all, why was he rushing away into the woods to carry a three-year-old when he didn't even care for children? He knew, of course, just why he was concerned. He hated to see someone as small as Lady Rosemary have to carry too heavy a load. He reminded himself that he had paused along a road in the hills of Italy to carry a load too heavy for the old woman struggling beneath its weight. This was no different.

And he increased his speed so that he could catch up with them before she was exhausted. There was no problem with following their tracks in the snow, and in the distance he could hear them singing. He paused a moment so that he could hear the melody over the crunching of the snow beneath his boots. It had been years since he had even thought about that carol, but it lifted his spirits to hear the familiar refrain of "The Holly and the Ivy" sounding sweetly through the crisp air:

The rising of the sun
And the running of the deer,
The playing of the merry organ,
Sweet singing in the choir.

He smiled to himself and hurried on, humming along with the carolers.

"Look, Rose! It's Aubrey's uncle!" piped Jamie, breaking into the song as he caught sight of Barrisford.

"Lord Barrisford!" exclaimed Rosemary in amazement. "I didn't realize that you were up or we would have invited you to come with us."

"Normally, of course, I would not arise before noon or go to bed before dawn," he said dryly, "but I thought that I would try to keep country hours while I am here. If I were to keep London hours, I might never see anyone else in the house." Not that that would be such a bad thing, he thought to himself. It could save him a great deal of inconvenience.

Rosemary regarded him closely, suspecting that more lay behind his words. He had seemed almost kind last night with Charlotte, but she distrusted his faint air of mockery. She was certain that he was scrutinizing her closely, and she was uncomfortable and resentful because of it.

Isabella, however, smiled at him gently. "We should hate not to see you, Lord Barrisford. We have been hoping that you will tell us some stories about London and about your travels. Aubrey says that you have been everywhere."

He bowed briefly to her. "Aubrey says more than he should. I have done some traveling, but not as much, I fear, as he would have you think."

"Still it would be delightful to hear about it, Lord Barrisford. Do promise that you will tell us about it."

"I would surely be a churl to refuse you, Lady Isabella," he said, smiling down at her. "I would count it a privilege."

"Don't you think, Bella, that you should stay at the Hall?" asked Rosemary anxiously, her thoughts diverted from her problem with Barrisford. Isabella's cheeks, usually so pale, now looked almost feverishly flushed. "Even though the sun is out, it is still very cold, and I am afraid that it will be too much for you."

Bella shook her head stubbornly. "We are only gathering the greens for the kissing bough and the mantels today," she reminded Rosemary. "That will not take us very long, and then I will sit quietly by the fireside for the rest of the day, Rose. You must stop worrying about me," she said gently. "I will be quite all right."

Rosemary gave it up. "Very well then. We will get this done as quickly as possible so that I can get you inside again."

Barrisford watched their exchange curiously.

He had not thought of it particularly, but now that his attention had been called to it, he could see that Lady Isabella most certainly was not as strong as the others. Indeed, she already appeared tired after so brief an exertion. Lady Anne linked her arm through her sister's, however, and they continued along the path.

Rosemary turned to go deeper into the woods, and Barrisford leaned down and took Charlotte from her arms. Rosemary looked up, startled, but he merely smiled and settled the little girl comfortably against his shoulder.

"It is easier for me," he said simply, and turned to go on.

"Rose! Anne! Wait for me!" called a voice from behind them, and Barrisford looked up to see the young man from the skating party hurrying toward them. "You know I wouldn't miss this for anything!"

The introductions that had been neglected last night were made now and Barrisford noted with amusement that Julian's bow was just stiff enough to let him know that he really was not welcome. Once that was past, Julian gave his attention to Rosemary, leaving Anne and Isabella and the children to talk to Barrisford. He managed to hold Rosemary back a little behind the others so that he could speak to her alone, thinking their conversation would be masked by the noise of the children. Barrisford, however, even though appearing not to do so, was listening intently.

"You can't do it, Rose," Julian was saying in a low, intense voice. "I told you from the beginning that you couldn't do it."

"You are mistaken, Julian," she replied calmly. "It is the only possible thing for me to do, and you would recognize that if you would only be sensible."

"Sensible! Rose, you know that I love you. We've been through this all before. Just give me permission to do something about it."

She shook her head. "It won't do, Julian," she said decisively. Now be a good boy and help me find the greens for the kissing bough. Let's see that the children have a good time."

His expression made it clear that his heart was not in it, but he did his best to make his countenance cheerful and turned to the rest of the group. It was obvious to Barrisford that he was a favored companion, long used to their company. He and Robert made snowballs and pelted the others with them, then one another. He followed Jamie off the path and more deeply into the trees to look for rabbit tracks. He sang carols with the ladies. He and Lady Anne together found the holly and mistletoe that they were searching for and began clipping it for the baskets, and he good-naturedly climbed into any tree that they pointed out to him.

Altogether, thought Barrisford, it was a cheerful family outing. Tempers were good, even those of the children, whom he was ac-

111

customed to thinking of as quarrelsome little beasts. His experience with children had been limited, viewing them from afar with considerable distaste, disliking the whining and fussing he had seen in families of some of his married friends.

He considered himself a fair man, and he was willing to concede that it was successful chiefly because of Lady Rosemary. Although she was not the heart and soul of the party, it was she who quietly saw to it that everyone was involved, that Julian was not allowed to fall into the mopes, that Isabella had a comfortable place to sit and watch the others gathering.

He thought of what Webster MacLean had told him of her life. It seemed an extraordinary thing to him that a woman so young should have borne the responsibility of so many others for the length of time that he had indicated. Studying the group, he would have to say that she had been quite successful. Her charges all seemed cheerful, well cared for, and well mannered. And of course there were the cousins and Uncle Webster, apparently all her responsibility as well. He had not missed the general shabbiness of the Hall, or the fact that, although their gowns were clean and neat, they were far from stylish. Thinking of what he had known about Jack Trevelyan's spendthrift ways, he wondered how Lady Rosemary had managed it all.

Their baskets were soon filled, and they

112

turned their steps back to the Hall, invading Mrs. O'Ryan's kitchen to sit by the fire and prepare their greenery. The spicy fragrance of gingerbread filled the room, and they were soon all supplied with that delicacy of childhood, and mugs of hot cider as well.

"Does this remind you of your childhood days, Lord Barrisford?" asked Rosemary cheerfully, determined to make this silent, rather cynical man a part of the group. After all, judging by Aubrey's fondness of him, she would be seeing him quite often after their marriage.

"I am afraid not, Lady Rosemary," he returned dryly. "The servants always took care of any decorations that we had. I don't recall having much to do with it—or of being interested in it one way or another."

The rest of them looked shocked. "But that's terrible!" exclaimed Isabella. "This is one of the pleasantest times of the year. Do you not enjoy it now?"

He shrugged. "Not particularly," he admitted. "It holds no special charms for me. There are parties, of course, but those go on year round."

"Oh, I don't mean just parties—I mean everything that goes with the season," Bella responded urgently. "The mood—the happiness—the way everything looks at Christmas." She looked at the book in her lap. "Have you ever read Sir Walter Scott's 'Merry Christmas'?" she asked.

Robert groaned good-naturedly. "I knew she

113

would get to Sir Walter Scott. If there's a chance at all, she'll drag him into every conversation."

Isabella, accustomed to his teasing, ignored him and opened to her poem and read it to them in her gentle voice.

On Christmas Eve the bells were rung,
On Christmas Eve the mass was sung;
  The damsel donned her kirtle sheen,
The hall was dressed with holly green;
  Forth to the wood did merry-men go,
To gather in the mistletoe:

Then drink to the holly berry,
  With hey down, hey down derry!
The mistletoe we'll pledge also,
  And at Christmas all be merry,
At Christmas all be merry.

The fire, with well-dried logs supplied,
Went roaring up the chimney wide;
  Then came the merry masquers in,
And carols roared with blithesome din.
  England is merry England, when
Old Christmas brings his sports again.

She looked at him shyly when she had finished. "Don't you ever long to feel as he does in the poem?"

"Only when you read it, Lady Isabella," he responded gallantly.

"Perhaps you will feel differently about it after you spend Christmas with the Trevelyans, Lord Barrisford," said Julian, a little dryly. "It doesn't sound as though you have kept Christmas quite the way they do here."

Thinking that this was undoubtedly the case, Barrisford gave no indication that he planned to be gone from Marston Hall by Christmas Day. Nor that he intended to have Aubrey with him. In fact, looking around the kitchen at the cheerful, unassuming group gathered there, he felt for the first time that he might be mistaken in his first opinion of Lady Rosemary Trevelyan. When Amelia had first told him of the engagement, he had assumed that Lady Rosemary would turn out to be a beautiful, greedy young woman. Beautiful she certainly was, but he had seen little sign of greed.

He had been watching her behavior with Julian Melrose closely since overhearing their conversation, and, as nearly as he could tell, her manner had been perfectly natural and pleasant, not loverlike at all. Nor had he been able to detect any sign of the devoted lover in Melrose. Had he not heard them speaking, he would never have suspected that they were anything more than friends.

Now the two of them and Anne sat at the table, working on the hoops for the kissing

115

bough, closely supervised by the cousins and Charlotte. Julian thrust one hoop through the other and then they carefully garlanded each of the ribs with holly or ivy. Lady Anne had polished several red-cheeked apples and she hung them within it. Then they secured red candles around the hemisphere of the globular structure and hung a bunch of mistletoe from the bottom of it, decorating it with scarlet ribbons. Well satisfied with their work, they held it up for the others to admire.

"Where shall we hang it this year?" asked Candace.

"Not in my kitchen again," called Mrs. O'Ryan. "I need to work in here and there was too much kissing going on last year."

"We'll put it by the staircase in the great hall," decided Anne. "Since we have guests, we'll be using that room more than we usually do."

Accordingly, they all trooped to the front of the hall and carefully hung the bough in a strategic spot.

"No one will notice it until they're directly under it," observed John with satisfaction.

"Who are you going to catch there?" demanded Robert. He was younger by just a year and he felt it his responsibility to give John trouble whenever he could arrange it. "Do you still have your eye on Kate Macklin?" he inquired innocently. "Perhaps she'll be coming over to skate soon, and you can invite her in

116

here, and just casually say 'Kate, could you come here a moment?' And there you'll be—just standing there under the kissing bough, waiting."

A brotherly thump helped him to decide that he would do no more teasing for the moment, and the adults were able to step back and inspect their work.

"Let's just test it, Candace," said Julian suddenly, hustling the protesting Candace under it and kissing her soundly. "There! The kissing bough is officially open for business." He stood under the mistletoe suggestively, winking at the others and waiting for someone to kiss him.

"Oh, all right, Julian," conceded Rosemary. "You've won." And she gave him a sisterly peck on the cheek. At Julian's invitation, the rest of the ladies lined up to salute him.

"You should take advantage of a good thing, Lord Barrisford," he said, releasing Cousin Merriweather. It seemed to Barrisford that this was in the nature of a challenge, so he rose to the occasion.

"Perhaps I should," he conceded, and to the amusement of others, he picked up Charlotte and carried her under the bough, kissing her gently on the cheek. Looking at Rosemary over Charlotte's tousled curls, he smiled and added, "Of course, I do not feel that I must limit myself to one kiss. Charlotte and I are not try-

117

ing to be exclusive—any of the other ladies are welcome to join us."

Rosemary looked quickly down, trying to avoid his gaze, but Robert gave her a push, saying, "Go ahead, Rose! It's Christmas—and it's not sociable to ignore a guest!"

Thinking that she would have a little talk with Robert about the value of silence, Rosemary was still not able to look directly at Barrisford, but laughed lightly and replied easily enough, "I'm sure that Lord Barrisford does not wish to be surrounded by a covey of young girls."

"You wrong me, Lady Rosemary," he replied gravely, although his eyes were shining with amusement "I can think of nothing I would like better."

Before it was necessary for her to respond, Bella stepped forward quickly and kissed Barrisford lightly on the cheek, blushing as she did so.

"Thank you, Bella," he said in surprise. "It was very kind of you to rescue me from my kissless state."

Bella's kiss was followed by salutes from Merriweather and the twins amid noisy, mirthful comments from Robert and John, and Rosemary was relieved to escape the room before attention could be directed towards her again.

The rest of the day passed quietly enough,

with Julian staying for dinner quite as a matter of course.

"Do we skate tomorrow, Rose?" he asked at the table that evening.

"Oh, yes," she responded. "The children have friends coming for the afternoon, and we will all be down at the lake. Will you come, Julian?"

"You know that I will. There is no telling how long this will last and I would like to get in as much skating as I can."

Lady Rosemary turned to Barrisford, who had been listening quietly. "Julian is a wonderful skater, Lord Barrisford. I hope that you will come down and join us, too. Perhaps Aubrey will be back by then."

"I would be delighted to join you," he answered, noting with pleasure that Julian looked a little put out by his response. "I am afraid that I am not such an accomplished skater, however. I have been on the ice only a few times and I was not a notable success."

"There is really nothing to it, Lord Barrisford," Julian informed him a little loftily. "All that you need is a proper sense of balance to do the thing—and of course you must be able to move lightly. I would be happy to give you a few pointers."

"Julian is very modest, as you see," responded Rosemary, quelling him with a glance. "We would be happy to have you come if only so that he could give someone else a few pointers. It would give the rest of us a chance to skate without having to stop every few moments for a lesson."

"Very well," laughed her victim, throwing up his hands. "I promise that I won't offer anyone my expert advice tomorrow. We will all just enjoy ourselves."

If Barrisford reflected that he would scarcely have thought that skating with a gaggle of children and young misses would constitute an afternoon of enjoyment, he heroically refrained from saying so.

Dinner had been held particularly early that evening so that Julian could get himself home while he was still able to see, commenting that it wouldn't do to lame his favorite horse by falling into some snow-covered hole. The others seemed occupied with their own affairs, and so Barrisford took advantage of the moment to retire to the privacy of his own chamber and think. The fire had been lighted, and he was quite contented with no other light except the flickering flames.

He was, despite himself, quite taken with Lady Rosemary. Having watched her with her family, he had begun to feel that their suspicions were nothing more than that—groundless suspicions, and he wondered if he should interfere as he had planned. Perhaps he would merely offer Aubrey his congratulations upon his return and then take himself back to London to inform Amelia that she was about to

acquire a virtuous and lovely daughter-in-law—
with his blessing.

He smiled to himself at the thought of what
his sister would have to say to him. Thinking
of the difference in temperament between
Amelia and Lady Rosemary, he could only applaud his nephew's choice. Even if he did live
his life in the midst of countless relatives and
hangers-on, he would still live it in a happier
manner than he had thus far. He found himself wondering what life might have been like
for him had he found such an admirable
woman.

Strolling to his darkened window, he stared
down across the park and the lake and the
woods alongside them, all growing blurred in
the lavender shadows of twilight. He had
started to turn away when he saw a small figure wrapped in a cloak down at the lakeside.
He recognized the way she moved, and knew
that it was Lady Rosemary. He frowned. It was
very late to be skating, but she appeared to
be leaning over and adjusting the straps on
her skates.

He watched as she skated quickly across the
ice and, to his amazement, met someone who
was approaching from around the bend in the
lake. They linked arms and, moving swiftly,
glided from his sight around the bend, and in
an instant, his high opinion of Lady Rosemary
vanished. He had no doubt that she was meeting a lover. It was a strange place for an as-

signation to be sure, but the Hall scarcely offered any privacy so her choices must have been slender.

Pulling a chair to the window, he settled there to wait for her return. Some thirty minutes later, after darkness had fallen completely, he saw a small dot of light moving across the ice. It was Lady Rosemary, returning alone with a lighted lantern.

He closed the draperies slowly and walked back to the fire, deep in thought. So Lady Rosemary was not quite the saint that he had begun to think her. It was almost a relief. Her behavior was, in fact, exactly what he would expect of a woman. It pleased him to think that he need not revise his opinion after all.

He could see that he would have to rescue Aubrey after all. He decided that he would indeed attend the skating party the next day so that he could brush up on his skating—and acquire a pair of skates. When dusk fell tomorrow, he would be ready. He would discover just who Lady Rosemary's lover was and force Aubrey to face the truth about her. It was time to scotch her little plan.

Eight

Before luncheon the next day, Aubrey had arrived from his journey to Liverpool. He was delighted to find Barrisford in residence, and could not wait to hear his uncle's opinion of his bride-to-be.

"She is extraordinary, is she not?" he demanded proudly as they sat together in the library after they had dined.

"She is very unusual," his uncle conceded, reflecting that she was in one respect at least, very much like every other woman he had ever known—duplicitous.

"I knew that you would like her once you met her," returned Aubrey. "Since my mother is not going to be here for the marriage, I am glad that you will be able to tell her yourself that she is mistaken in her fears."

Barrisford debated with himself as to whether or not this was the moment to bring up Lady Rosemary's evening excursion, but decided that he would wait until he followed her tonight and had something more concrete to tell Aubrey.

"And so you have decided to claim your fortune, Aubrey," he remarked casually. "You realize that it was not necessary to marry in order to separate yourself from your mother and Barron, don't you? There was no need to take such a desperate step. I had told you that you might set up your own household at any time, you know."

"Yes, I am aware, Uncle, of how simple a matter you thought that would be. We differed on that point—but by marrying, I will have separated myself once and for all. Doing it now as I change my station in life seemed the reasonable thing to do. It is a time for changes."

He hesitated a moment, looking at Barrisford's enigmatic expression. "And quite apart from that, Uncle, although I had decided before I came here that I would offer for one of Jack Trevelyan's daughters if it were at all possible—once I was here and saw Rosemary, I knew that that was what I *wished* to do, not merely what I must do."

When Barrisford remained silent, he added, "You do think that she is lovely, don't you?"

Barrisford nodded. That much at least he could agree with. "She is certainly that, Aubrey. But you need not come here to find loveliness. London can supply beautiful young women by the dozen."

"Not like Rosemary," he returned with conviction. "I do not believe that there are many who can manage as capably as she does, nor who are as kind."

His uncle was forced to concede at least the first point. "I can see that she is accustomed to ruling the roast, Aubrey. Have you considered that she may wish to continue to do so?"

Aubrey laughed. "We shall get on together very well. She has been very happy to have me help her."

"A pocket lined with gold is always welcome," returned Barrisford dryly. "Perhaps she would not feel the same way if you were a poor man."

Aubrey flushed. "Why should I not help her when I have the power to do so?" he demanded. "My mother and Barron are forever saying to me that no one is interested in me, only in my money, that I should trust no one! Well, I am very weary of living in such a manner, Uncle! Since you are a wealthy man yourself, you should know how it feels!"

"I do indeed, Aubrey. That is why I am saying this to you. I could not count the number of women who have thrown themselves at my head because they had a mind to share my fortune."

"You are quite out there. Lady Rosemary did not throw herself at my head, as you so gracefully put it. I was the one who pressed her. And I tell you flatly, Uncle, that I will not hear her spoken of in such a manner. You have only to look at her family to know that you are wrong in your speculations. And I *shall* marry her, regardless of what any of you might say to me!"

Barrisford was startled by Aubrey's outburst, for the boy had always allowed himself to be guided, paying special attention to his uncle's words and prizing his advice. It was disconcerting, and it meant that it would take a bit more effort to disengage him from the lovely Lady Rosemary, but it was heartening, too. It was about time that the boy showed some spirit.

He changed the subject abruptly to another that had been troubling him. "What took you to Liverpool, Aubrey?"

This diversion was successful, for he had been eager to tell his uncle about his journey.

"I received an anonymous message that was simply directed to the heir of John Trevelyan, Duke of Stedham, and it stated that the writer had seen the emerald ring always worn by the late duke. It was in the window of a pawnshop in Liverpool. I suppose the writer thought that I would wish to reclaim it—and, of course, I would, for the sake of his family, not for myself."

"I recall that ring," Barrisford said slowly. "It was quite an unusual piece—a magnificent square-cut emerald in a very intricate setting. Stedham always wore it—I think it was one of the few things that he never staked at the gambling table." He looked at his nephew keenly. "And so you felt that this was urgent enough to leave here and make the journey to Liverpool."

"It isn't just because of that, uncle," Aubrey admitted slowly. "What troubled me was what Lady Rosemary had said about it. When she showed me the portraits in the long gallery, there was one done of her father some twenty years ago—and he was, of course, wearing the ring. When I commented upon what a handsome piece it was, she agreed, and said that he always wore it."

Barrisford looked at him questioningly, waiting for him to continue.

"Well, don't you see, Uncle, that if he always wore it, and if he was indeed washed overboard, the ring would have disappeared with him. Since it apparently didn't, it must have been taken before he went overboard—if that is indeed what happened—and since he wouldn't have parted with it willingly, it led me to wonder if there might have been foul play. And so, of course, I felt that I should look into the matter both because I am his heir and because I plan to marry his daughter."

Barrisford looked at his nephew in amazement. Never before had Aubrey undertaken any matter on his own initiative; he had always allowed others to guide his thoughts and actions. In spite of himself, he was impressed, and chalked this up to Lady Rosemary's influence. Perhaps this whole experience would do Aubrey a great deal of good.

"There was something else, too, Uncle. I recalled that when Crispin, Stedham's man of business, came to call upon me immediately after the duke's disappearance, he told me that he had dire misgivings when he met the captain of the ship from which the duke had disappeared. He was apparently of such questionable appearance that Crispin distrusted him at the time, although he could find nothing missing from among his master's possessions."

"And what did you hope to accomplish by going to Liverpool?"

"Well, I planned to reclaim the ring, of course, but then I wished to discover who had taken it to the pawnshop and see if I could trace him."

"And what happened?"

Aubrey sighed. "When I reached the pawnshop, the ring was gone. The proprietor said that a middle-aged man had claimed it—and he said that he did not know his name. Nor could he remember who had brought it in. It seemed to me that his memory was a most convenient one, and I tried to press him, but nothing came of my questions."

"Then what did you do?" asked Barrisford, fascinated by this new view of his nephew.

"I made the rounds of all the pawnshops I

could find, checking to see if it might turn up. I had no luck, of course, but I left messages in all of them with my London address, asking to be informed should it appear."

"I am impressed by your thoroughness," said Barrisford admiringly. "I had no idea that you could handle affairs so capably, Aubrey."

"Why should you have known?" demanded his nephew. "When have I ever been given an opportunity to do so?"

Not giving Barrisford an opportunity to reply, he went on. "And then I went down to the docks, and, fortunately, the ship on which Stedham had traveled was there, and I was able to question the captain."

"Did you discover anything?" asked Barrisford curiously, more and more amazed by this change in his docile nephew.

Aubrey shook his head. "No more than Crispin had already told me—that Captain Bing looks the part of a rogue but seems to have done nothing amiss. When I asked him about the ring, he said he remembered it, of course, but that as far as he knew, Stedham had been wearing it when he went overboard."

"Did he have the same crew with him?" inquired Barrisford

"According to Captain Bing, only one had left abruptly when they reached Liverpool."

"Then that could be your man. He could have jumped ship, pawned the ring, and left for parts unknown."

Aubrey nodded. "I believe that may be exactly what happened," he agreed. "The captain gave me his name, and I made inquiries along the docks and with some of the other captains, but no one seemed to have heard of him."

"I would say, Aubrey, that you have done everything that can be done at this point—and done it very well. All that you can do now is wait to see if you hear from any of the pawnshops about the reappearance of the ring."

Barrisford's praise brought a flush to the young man's cheeks. He felt that he did merit some part of the praise, and that made him more grateful than ever to the Trevelyans. Had it not been for meeting them after Stedham's death, he might still be sitting in London, his every move questioned by Barron and his mother. And he knew that he would never again live in such a manner.

Nine

Rosemary had mixed feelings upon Aubrey's arrival. She needed now to again assume her role of fiancée, being attentive to Aubrey and allowing him to make the decisions. These were not welcome changes for her, but she felt that she could make them gracefully since doing so would benefit her family. She was also relieved to have him back again because he would take Lord Barrisford off her hands.

Barrisford had made her extremely uneasy. She knew that he was studying her every move, trying to determine what manner of person she was. There had been moments yesterday when she thought he almost approved of her, when, indeed, she thought he might actually like her. Then she would be exposed to a chilly gaze that dissipated any thought of approval. He was a most unaccountable man, she thought—charming when he wished to be, careless of what others thought—not at all of the same disposition as his easygoing nephew.

At least, she told herself, she was marrying Aubrey and not his uncle. She did not doubt that Aubrey would cater to her wishes and treat her well. Barrisford would be quite another story. Of course, she thought, had Barrisford been the heir, there would have been no problem because she obviously would not have caught his eye as she had Aubrey's. His uncle was too world-weary and experienced to be charmed by some country miss. She hoped that she could at least persuade him to like her, or being a part of Aubrey's family was going to be very uncomfortable indeed.

Rosemary was looking forward to the afternoon skating party, not only because the children were excited but also because it would bring in some outsiders to lighten the atmosphere a little. Barrisford's presence had introduced a tension that made her uneasy. It seemed to be affecting no one else, but even with Aubrey's return—and he had explained his trip simply by saying it was an urgent business matter—she felt restless. Barrisford was watching them both.

A day for a skating party could not have been better chosen, she reflected later, watching the skaters gathering at the edge of the lake. The day was crisp and cold, the sun bright in a flawless blue sky, the snow still fresh and white and sparkling. They had arranged benches around a blazing fire so that the skaters would have a place to strap on their skates in comfort as well as a place to thaw while circulation returned to their cold-numbed noses and hands and feet. Mrs. O'Ryan and Uncle Webster had brought down a huge pot of steaming hot chocolate and placed it on a flat rock carefully arranged at the edge of the fire.

The children and their friends, their bright scarves and mittens flashes of color against the backdrop of white and gray and black, raced across the ice, devising new games as they went. Julian was there, of course, skating gracefully with Anne; Uncle Webster, his pipe firmly between his teeth, was studiously making his way around the edge, moving at a slow, dignified pace, avoiding the youngsters. To her surprise, she saw Lord Barrisford strap a pair of skates to his boots, ease carefully onto the ice, and glide quite gracefully to join Uncle Webster.

"Did you know, my lord," said Uncle Webster, removing his pipe and inclining his head toward Barrisford in greeting, "that there was once a battle fought on the ice?"

Barrisford laughed, prepared for anything. He had noticed that Webster had a taste for obscure bits of knowledge and enjoyed sharing them with others.

Uncle Webster nodded. "In 1572, the Dutch fleet was frozen in at Amsterdam, and the Spanish attacked across the ice, using spiked clogs. But the Dutch were more clever still, for they put on their skates and took to the ice, routing the Spaniards. They say that the Duke of Alva was so impressed by them that he ordered seven thousand pairs of skates for his soldiers."

"And did he use them?" asked Barrisford.

Uncle Webster allowed himself a dry smile and shook his head. "After a year, when they still couldn't skate in formation, he gave up the notion." He drew thoughtfully on his pipe. "Napoleon did some skating, too—but he didn't attempt to train his soldiers to do so."

Barrisford had been noting the easy glide of the older man, far more graceful than his own. "You look as though you have done a fair amount of skating yourself, Mr. MacLean."

"I have skated since I was very young, and when I was a young man at the university, I belonged to the Edinburgh skating club, the first one of its kind."

They skated on in easy silence for a moment, enjoying the day and the pleasant vision of Rosemary and Aubrey gliding ahead of them, arms linked. That couple was soon joined by Julian and Anne, and the sound of laughter drifted back to the pair behind them.

"Julian Melrose seems very much at his ease here," observed Barrisford.

"He is considered one of the family. I understand that it has always been that way. He is normally here several times a week unless he is called away on business. I have heard

Candace say that he would be better off just to take up residence here. Now that the lake is frozen, he need not even saddle his horse to come, he can simply skate over."

"Can he indeed?" This much had captured Barrisford's interest.

"The lake lies on both properties, so it is an easy matter—and, as you can see, Julian is an excellent skater. He enjoys the exercise."

"How very interesting," murmured Barrisford, thinking of the previous evening, and silence reigned again for a few minutes.

"Lady Rosemary seems to possess a pleasant disposition," Barrisford remarked in an off-hand manner, watching with interest as the couples traded partners, Anne now with Aubrey, Julian with Rosemary.

"I have never known anyone with a better," agreed Uncle Webster. "Isabella is the only one who can equal her for sweetness of temperament, but of course Isabella has less to try her. It is easy enough to be pleasant when everything goes as you would wish for it to. I have noticed that Rosemary does not lose her pleasant ways even when everything turns against her."

"You are a loyal friend and family member," said Barrisford, smiling a little at this description.

"I am speaking no more than the truth, young man," said Uncle Webster stiffly, forgetting for the moment that he was speaking to

135

an earl. "I daresay that you, for instance, have not faced as many disasters in your lifetime as she has faced in hers. And she has never given way in the face of them. She is still cheerful, still concerned about those about her, still certain that things can be worked out. She doesn't spend her time blaming herself or others. She simply sets about correcting the problem."

Barrisford thought of her recent fortuitous betrothal and smiled again. "I would agree with you, Mr. MacLean, that she is a very resourceful young woman."

Looking around the lake, his eyebrows drew together a little. Their conversation had reminded him of Lady Isabella, and it occurred to him that he had seen the rest of the household, but that there had been no sign of her.

"Does Lady Isabella not skate?" he inquired abruptly.

Uncle Webster shook his head. "She always has, but since her illness last spring, she has been quite weak. I imagine the cold and the exertion together would be too much for her. And it is a pity, for she loves skating." He pointed back to the lake's edge. "She is there by the fire, keeping warm. I heard her say that she wanted to at least watch for a little while."

Leaving Uncle Webster, Barrisford skated back to the fire and joined Lady Isabella in a cup of chocolate. A few minutes later, he reappeared on the ice, holding Isabella securely.

"Now, Lady Isabella, you will scarcely know that you are skating and I won't allow you to grow at all tired," he told her encouragingly. "We shall just make one turn around this portion of the lake and then I will take you back to the fire and tell you of my travels."

Rosemary was startled to see Bella on the ice, and still more struck by the identity of her partner. Julian was immediately irate and ready to take Barrisford to task for endangering Isabella's health. Rosemary caught his sleeve before he could do so, however.

"Look at her, Julian. She is delighted to be out once again. Perhaps I was wrong to try to keep her from skating."

"Nonsense, Rose," he growled. "You know how quickly she becomes worn down. Barrisford is giving no thought to her health. And look at the way he is holding her!"

Barrisford was not skating with arms linked. Instead, he had placed one arm firmly about Isabella's waist and taken one of her hands securely in his own, leaving her free to keep her pelisse from catching on her skates. Isabella, delighted to be on the ice again, followed his instructions confidently. Barrisford seemed to her a very capable man, and his kindness to her had already won her.

"Don't be such a bear, Julian. He is keeping her from exerting herself anymore than necessary and from falling. A little bit of exercise will probably do her no harm, so we shall watch to see how this goes."

Barrisford was as good as his word. After one careful trip around the section of the lake that could be seen from Marston Hall, he led Isabella back to the fire and unstrapped her skates for her. As he was settling her comfortably to have a cup of chocolate before returning her to the Hall, Julian and Rosemary joined them.

"Did you enjoy your skating, Bella?" asked Rosemary, anxiously searching her sister's face for signs of undue fatigue. Instead, there was a faint color there that she had not seen for months.

"Oh, yes, indeed!" exclaimed Isabella. "It was very kind of Lord Barrisford to think of me."

"It was my pleasure, Lady Isabella," he remarked courteously, bowing to her. "May I have the pleasure of your company now, Lady Rosemary?" he inquired.

Startled by his request, she nodded briefly. There was nothing she wished to do less than skate with this man and be forced to make conversation with him, but she could do nothing but consent.

Barrisford turned to Isabella. "I will join you again shortly, Lady Isabella, after you have rested. Then I shall walk you back to the Hall and tell you some of my travel tales if they will not bore you."

"Of course they won't, Lord Barrisford," she responded, glowing. "I should love to hear them."

Leaving Julian to watch them broodingly, they returned to the ice. Rosemary stiffened as he took her hand, wondering if he was going to hold her in the same manner he had held Bella. It had been forgivable then, for Bella needed his support. She, however, needed no such thing.

Noting her reaction, he smiled down at her mockingly. "You need not fear, Lady Rosemary. I am not going to put my arm around you—tempting though it is." Ignoring the sudden rise of color in her already rosy cheeks, he reached out and took both her hands in his.

"I am not as adept a skater as you, Lady Rosemary, and I find it easier to skate with a partner like this."

Rosemary, who did not believe his humble words for a moment, responded tartly, "I would prefer to skate unaided, Lord Barrisford," and attempted to remove her hands from his grasp.

"That would be most unkind of you, Lady Rosemary," he reproached her. "You would be placing *me* at risk—and since I have heard your kindness lauded since I crossed the threshold of Marston Hall, I must rely upon your good nature."

They were already moving rather swiftly

across the ice, and she knew that jerking her hands loose from his firm grip—aside from being rather a ridiculous and childish gesture—was very likely to send her spinning across the ice. Since she had no desire to be plucked from another snowbank, she bowed to the inevitable and forced herself to smile.

"I am afraid, my lord, that you must not rely upon my good nature. It comes and goes at will."

"I shall consider myself warned," he assured her. "Does it come and go with everyone—or just with particularly annoying people?"

"Just with particularly annoying people," she returned briskly. "But I feel quite sure that you do not trouble yourself about whether or not you are annoying. I see that you are accustomed to having your own way—"

"How observant you are," he interrupted admiringly, which wrung a reluctant laugh from her, although she continued immediately.

"—and you run roughshod over others without giving it a second thought," she finished.

He looked genuinely surprised. "What would make you say such a thing as that, Lady Rosemary?" he inquired. "Over whom have I trampled?"

"Isabella for one," she replied briskly, conveniently forgetting that she had just reprimanded Julian for finding fault with Barrisford's behavior. "She was not supposed to skate; it could be dangerous for her to exert herself. But you insisted upon it, I am sure, and Bella gave way to your wishes. I should imagine that everyone always does."

"Are you thinking of Aubrey?" he asked directly. "Do you think he will do anything that I wish?"

She was surprised by his frankness, but she returned it. "I should imagine that, since he thinks you are quite wonderful and since you are so much older, he would do as you wish in the twinkling of an eye."

"So much older!" he exclaimed, nettled in spite of himself. "Young lady, how old do you suppose I am?"

Pleased to have annoyed him, she inspected him smilingly, enjoying his discomfiture, and deliberately advanced his age. "I should imagine about forty-five or fifty," she responded demurely.

"Well, I am not! I am—" He broke off, eyeing her suspiciously. "Making a May-game of me, are you, Lady Rosemary?" he inquired gently. "Well, it will not work. I do remember what we were speaking of. Undoubtedly you were speaking the truth when you said that Aubrey would do as I wished in a moment."

Her eyes clouded a little as she looked up at him, for they both understood that he was speaking of taking Aubrey from Marston Hall and breaking their engagement. "You are here to have him cry off, aren't you, my lord?" she asked bluntly.

He paused a moment before answering. "Yes," he responded slowly, "but, to be quite honest, I am not certain that I can change his mind now. It seems to me that Aubrey has changed a great deal in a very small measure of time."

She was surprised by his response, and they skated on silently. Without noticing it, she had grown accustomed to his manner of holding her, so she was surprised to encounter an angry look from Julian as he and Anne swept past. She tried gently to remove her hands from his grip, but he showed no sign of noticing her attempts and so she relinquished her efforts.

"And I think, Lady Rosemary, that the changes have come about because of you."

She looked at him in surprise. She had been aware of no changes in Aubrey, of course, and she wondered if the changes were good or bad. Probably bad, she thought to herself. And he is holding me responsible for them.

"I hear from everyone, Lady Rosemary," he continued blandly, "that you are not only kind, but also generous and clever and good—and willing to do anything for your family."

"My family is very important to me," she conceded, wondering if he was referring to her approaching marriage. As for the other things you said, they are not particularly true—no more so for me than for others."

"And modest, too," he said admiringly. "I

had no idea that you possessed all the virtues—and beauty, too. I suppose that you will tell me next that you are quite plain and that you do not think of attracting men."

Uncertain of what to say, Rosemary decided to remain silent. There had been a moment or two when she felt comfortable with him, indeed almost enjoyed him, but she could hear the mockery in his tone and knew that he was not her friend.

"I like plain dealing, Lady Rosemary," he said abruptly. "If you are marrying Aubrey to provide for your family, it is possible that we could come to some other arrangement that would solve your problem and leave Aubrey free."

Rosemary drew in a sharp breath as guilt flooded her. He was right, of course, that was exactly what she was doing. But she did not feel that she could trust him to keep his agreement—nor did she feel that she could accept it. To accept it would be very much like blackmail. At least she felt that in marrying Aubrey—if he truly wished to marry her—she was making a bargain. She was, in effect, promising to make him a good wife, and, in return, he would care for her family. Even though he was right about her motives, she could not stem a rush of anger at the thought he could believe that she could allow herself to be guilty of blackmail. Marriage was an honest bargain;

143

she would be, so to speak, paying for services rendered.

As she grew angrier, his nearness became unendurable and she jerked her hands from his. "I do not care to listen to you any longer, Lord Barrisford," she said frostily, and turned to skate away.

"No, I did not think you would face the truth," he called after her. She was exactly what he had thought. All of his instincts had been correct. He was angry and disgusted—and acutely aware that she was gone from his side.

Barrisford skated back to the fire and gently led Isabella back to the warmth of the Hall, making her comfortable beside the drawing room fire and delighting her with stories of the isles of Greece. Finally, though, the effects of her exertion began to tell and her eyelids began to droop. Apologizing profusely, she thanked him for his company and excused herself to go up to her chamber and rest until dinner.

Determined not to go to the lake again, Barrisford sat reading for a while in the library, but grew restless finally and paced about, thinking of the evening. He knew now where he could find a pair of skates and he would be watching this evening. It irritated him beyond belief that she should act so guileless when he knew perfectly well that she was playing a double game. It was galling, too, to realize that her lack of candor bothered him. He had almost allowed himself to be hoodwinked when he first met the family. It was fortunate for Aubrey that his uncle was experienced in the ways of women.

He strolled into the Great Hall just as Rosemary entered it. She stopped short when she saw him, then walked toward him, trying to speak casually.

"I was looking for Isabella, my lord. Have you seen her?"

"I wearied her with my travel tales and she went up to rest until dinner," he replied.

She turned toward the staircase, then forced herself to come back and hold out her hand to him. "I do wish to thank you, my lord, for being so kind to Isabella," she said stiffly. "We had not thought about allowing her to skate, and we should have done so. I—"

She did not finish her sentence. As she had walked back toward him, she had stepped under the kissing bough. Noticing it, Barrisford, angry with himself as well as Rosemary, caught her roughly to him and kissed her harshly. There was no pretense of tenderness—in fact, the kiss seemed more like an assault than a gesture of affection. When she tried to push him away, he simply held her so tightly against him that she was unable to move, and his hand cupped behind her head kept her from turning her face away. Despite herself, she found that she was yielding to his touch.

When he finally released her, it was difficult

to tell which of them was more shaken. Barrisford was furious with himself for his lack of control, but he told himself that she had most certainly invited such treatment. He prepared himself for her recriminations, but there were none. She stood perfectly still for a moment, trying to regain her breath and her composure. Her face was pale and her dark eyes angry.

"I should slap you, I know, Lord Barrisford," she said, measuring her words carefully. "But to do so, I should have to touch you." And she turned away abruptly and hurried up the stairs.

For a moment Barrisford felt only guilt, for she looked very young and vulnerable. Then, however, he reminded himself of her treatment of Aubrey and her lack of honesty, and he grew angry once again. He knew also that he had longed to touch her and that merely fueled his anger, for he had no desire to give any woman power over him again. He could not imagine what it would be like if Aubrey really did marry this young woman and brought her within the family. He would be forced to see her again and again—and as Aubrey's wife.

He intended to take Aubrey and to put Marston Hall as far behind both of them as possible. Tonight, if his luck was in, he would catch the fair Lady Rosemary with her lover and then convincing Aubrey that he had made a mistake would be child's play.

Twilight found Barrisford at his window watching the grounds below very carefully for any sign of movement. An hour passed and he resigned himself to the fact that he had either missed her or that she had not gone out that evening. It occurred to him, however, that there would be a full moon this evening, and he smiled. She would be going later. Accordingly, he straightened his neckcloth and went downstairs to the drawing room to join the others for coffee.

Lady Rosemary was there, and she served his coffee graciously, but without meeting his eyes, just as she had avoided speaking to him at dinner. Barrisford noticed that Lady Candace appeared to take note of this, but no one else seemed aware of any difference in her attitude. Still anxious to punish her for her duplicity, he decided to force her to speak to him.

"Has there been any activity under the kissing bough?" he inquired of the room at large in an interested tone. He was pleased to see that she looked at him then. Her head flew up at his words and her eyes caught his angrily.

The children had joined them, and it was Robert who answered him. "It is John that

147

you should be asking, Lord Barrisford," he said laughingly. "I saw him come this way with Kate Macklin this afternoon."

John's glance at Robert was almost as angry as Lady Rosemary's at him, Barrisford reflected. "You should learn to mind your own business, Robert," he snapped, his eyes flashing.

"You know that Robert doesn't mean anything by his remarks," Rosemary said soothingly. "He just wants to see you become angry, so don't give him the pleasure." And that is just the advice I should be giving myself, she thought in an abstracted way. She was certain that he was deliberately trying to upset her, and she was determined not to allow him to do so.

"Were you thinking of supplying some of the activity, Lord Barrisford?" she asked coolly.

"It would depend upon my partner," he responded, surprised by her calmness.

"Well, I think there should be some activity immediately," announced Aubrey. "I have yet to be kissed beneath it."

And pulling Rosemary to her feet, he walked resolutely to the door, and the others rose to follow them. Reluctantly Barrisford joined them, certain of what he would see.

Aubrey pulled Rosemary to him and kissed her gently under the mistletoe, applauded by the rest of the group. Isabella stood murmuring something as the applause died away, and

Robert called out, "Rose, Bella is quoting poetry again and you'd best beware! This time I think it's about you!"

He pulled Isabella into the center of the group and said, "Now then, Bella, say it for everyone to hear. You know that a poem is lost upon me."

There was more encouraging applause, and Isabella shyly began:

"As the holly groweth green
And never changeth hue,
So am I, ever hath been,
To my lady true.

As the holly groweth green
With ivy all alone,
When flower cannot be seen,
And greenwood leaves be gone:

Now unto my lady
Promise to her I make,
From all others only
To her I me betake."

She finished to the sound of applause, but Barrisford was heard to remark dryly, "Very suitable! That was supposedly written by Henry VIII—and we all know how true he was to each of his ladies!"

Everyone stared at him for a moment, startled by the barbed remark, then Aubrey laughingly asked, "Are you saying, then, Uncle, that I am like Henry VIII? You will frighten Rosemary away with comments like that."

"Oh, I don't think so," he responded dryly. "And although it is called 'To My Lady True,' it isn't only the gentleman who may betray as Henry did. Ladies have been known to do so, too." Again and again, he added to himself—and then was angry because he had allowed himself to speak his thoughts aloud.

Isabella looked stricken, and, seeing her expression, Aubrey threw his uncle an annoyed glance, then forced himself to smile.

"You must forgive him," Aubrey said swiftly, before the full import of his words could sink in. "My uncle has been too long a bachelor, and has become crotchety."

"Well, although I, too, have been a bachelor for many a day, I believe that I can think of a use for the kissing bough," said Uncle Webster, leading the conversation gently into more pleasant paths, and he led Cousin Matilda, blushing, to the mistletoe and kissed her soundly.

There was more applause, and then everyone took a turn, one by one, until they all had been under the bough and received their kisses except for Barrisford.

"Come along, Uncle," said Aubrey merrily. "I'm certain that if you stand here someone will take pity upon you."

Reluctantly, Barrisford took his place, glancing at Lady Rosemary as he did so. It was Cousin Merriweather and Charlotte who gave him his kisses, however, and he noticed that he could no longer catch Rosemary's eye. She was very resolutely looking away from him.

When he returned to his room, he extinguished the candles and returned again to his window, prepared to wait patiently for his quarry. As he had expected, she appeared on the moonlit snow below, and he hurried to follow her, prepared to skate all the way to Julian Melrose's house if necessary—for he was quite certain that Julian was the lover. As she approached the lake, she stopped several times, and he feared that she had heard him and was stopping to listen. However, she continued on, slipped into her skates, and glided onto the frozen surface.

At the edge of the lake he knelt in the shadows to strap on his skates, watching her carefully as she skated across its glistening center. As soon as he was ready, he, too, slipped onto the ice, keeping well within the shadows of the trees leaning low along its eastern boundary. Just as he had the night before, the man appeared from around the bend of the lake, linked arms with Rosemary, and skated with her around the bend and out of sight.

Barrisford began to pick up speed to try to catch up. To his dismay, however, he hit a rough patch of ice in the darkness. He felt his feet slipping out from under him and reached instinctively for one of the branches hanging out over the ice. It snapped in his hand, and the sharpness of the sound was like a pistol shot echoing across the ice in the clear night air.

Crouching low in the shadows, he waited to see if they would reappear, and, after what seemed an interminable wait, they did. Together they stole cautiously to the curve of the lake and peered carefully around it. Seeing nothing, the man turned and hurried away, gliding rapidly out of sight around the curve, while Lady Rosemary skated quickly across the brightly lit portion once more.

So hastily was she moving that there was no opportunity for Barrisford to follow her. Instead, he simply watched from his vantage point in the shadows. When she was almost in the center of their portion of the lake, something slipped from her muff and lay glittering on the ice. She was skating too quickly to notice her loss, and once she had disappeared in the direction of Marston Hall, Barrisford made his way to the center and picked it up. It was the ring with the square-cut emerald.

He stared at it for a moment, thinking of what Aubrey had told him about it, then took out his handkerchief and knotted the ring securely within it. Without a doubt it was Stedham's ring.

He smiled to himself. The question now was what he would do with it. He tucked it carefully within his waistcoat pocket and made his way slowly home, avoiding the moonlit areas, remembering that Lady Rosemary might go inside and then watch to see if she had been followed.

There was no question in his mind now: he had what he needed to prove Lady Rosemary's falseness.

Ten

The next morning at breakfast, Barrisford was pleased to note that Lady Rosemary was looking quite tense and pale. Nor was he the only one to notice her condition.

"Are you feeling quite the thing, Rosemary?" Aubrey asked in some concern.

She nodded briefly and attempted a smile. "My head aches a little, Aubrey. It is no more than that."

"We'll still be able to go for the rest of the Christmas greens, won't we?" John asked, his brow wrinkling.

Rosemary forced a smile. "Yes, of course, we will. After all, this is Christmas Eve. We'll go this afternoon."

Reassured, John returned his attention to his porridge and the other children began to make plans for the afternoon.

Rosemary excused herself shortly afterward, pleading her headache, and started upstairs to her chamber. Aubrey had asked her to stay with him, but she had replied that she would feel much more the thing after resting awhile.

"Rose doesn't rest," observed John to his older brother. "And she never has the headache. I wonder what's wrong."

Robert shrugged, but Barrisford smiled to himself. He knew precisely what was wrong. Lady Rosemary had discovered her loss and now she was trying to determine just where she might have left the ring. He patted his pocket, where it rested securely. Excusing himself, he followed her lightly up the stairs, wanting to be certain to keep an eye on her as she searched.

As he went quietly up the stairs, he heard voices from the landing above him, and he stood perfectly still so that he might hear what was said, for he suspected Rosemary of plotting with someone else.

"Are you certain, Rose, that you should be marrying Aubrey?" he heard Lady Candace ask in a low voice. "Is that what is troubling you?"

"No, no, of course not," she replied in an abstracted voice. "That is not a trouble at all."

"But you do care for him, do you not, Rose?" asked Lady Candace. "You must not marry him just for us if you do not care for him at all."

"No, it isn't that, Candace. He is a fine young man—of course, I care for him. You

155

need not worry yourself at all. And now I must go, my dear. . . ."

Candace went on as though she had not spoken. "It just seems to me that I have seen you look at Lord Barrisford as though there were something between you, and I thought perhaps—"

"Lord Barrisford is nothing to me, Candace," returned her sister in a low, tense voice. "I cannot think why you are going on about this when you know I am marrying Aubrey. I am fortunate that he is so kind and generous a man. You might offer me your pity were I marrying Lord Barrisford."

Barrisford heard her hurry up the rest of the steps and down the passageway. To his relief, Candace followed her slowly instead of turning to come back down the stairs. Thoughtfully he entered the drawing room, fingering the ring in his pocket, and walked to a window that overlooked the lake.

He allowed himself to think for a moment of what Candace had said, that Rosemary had looked at him as though there were something between them. And there is, he thought grimly: distrust—and, on her part at least, dislike. He had enough pride to feel the sting of her parting words to Candace. He had always considered himself a gentleman, but it was obvious that she felt Aubrey was more well bred than his uncle.

What she thought was really of no great consequence to him, of course. He shrugged off such extraneous matters and focused on the real problem: the appearance of the ring. It seemed unlikely that she could have arranged for her own father's death, but it was obvious that she intended to profit by it. How did she come to have her father's ring, a ring that would not have left his hand while he lived?

He wondered for a moment—could she have arranged her father's death so that she could save the rest of the family from ruin? It was well known that Jack Trevelyan had been busily squandering what was left of the family fortune. Indeed, Barrisford had only to look about him at Marston Hall to see the effects of years of poor management. It would have been a relief to the family to know that such depredations were at an end. Of course, it would have meant losing Marston Hall, too. Lady Rosemary could not have been absolutely positive that she would be able to ensnare the new heir as she had. So it would have been a great risk. Too farfetched, probably, to be possible.

Watching from behind a curtain, he saw her start down toward the lake, just as he had suspected she would when she could not find the ring in her room or on the stairs. She had slipped a dark cloak over her clothes and was hurrying down to the ice, skates in hand. Barrisford lost no time in joining her, pleased to see her irritated expression as he sat down next to her to strap his skates on. She quickly finished adjusting hers and rose.

"You must forgive me for being such a poor hostess, my lord," she said coldly, "but I really have no desire for company just now." And she stepped onto the ice and started away from him.

Swiftly he finished fastening the straps and a few long strides placed him beside her; then he linked her unwilling arm through his. "I am concerned about you, Lady Rosemary," he returned pleasantly. "You look too pale and I am afraid that you might suddenly feel faint were you left alone."

She looked at him suspiciously. "I am quite all right, thank you," she replied stiffly, still trying to disengage her arm and move away from him.

"There is no point in trying to get away, Lady Rosemary," he said grimly. "I have something that may help your headache." He looked down at her delicate face for a moment. "Or perhaps it may make it worse," he amended.

And, to her outrage, he placed one arm tightly around her waist, firmly anchoring her right arm under his, and took her left hand in his.

"Lord Barrisford, release me immediately!" she demanded through clenched teeth. "I am not Isabella, and I need no help from you!"

"Indeed you are not Isabella—insofar as I

can tell, she is a gentle and trustworthy young woman," he returned coldly. "And I assure you that I held her far more tenderly."

Rosemary had no trouble believing this, for he had so tight a grip that she could scarcely breathe, and he had increased their speed until they were virtually racing across the ice toward the bend in the lake.

"I do not wish to be held at all!" she exclaimed. "Tenderly, or otherwise! You must let me go!' "

An upward glance at his grim expression informed her that her words were wasted.

"Do not flatter yourself that I *wish* to be holding you like this. It is merely the most expedient thing to do."

Nothing more was said until he had skated her around the bend and out of the sight of the Hall. Then, still holding her firmly with his right arm, he took the ring from his pocket and held it in front of her.

"Would you care to explain this, Lady Rosemary?" he demanded. "Who were you meeting last night? How did you come by the ring?" He waited impatiently for her response, but she merely held out her hand for the ring and said nothing.

Finally, when he returned the ring to his pocket and she saw there was no choice, Rosemary explained.

"It was Julian's bailiff who found it in a pawnshop in Liverpool," she said in a low

159

voice. Barrisford had expected that response, but he found his anger rising beyond his control. So it was Julian Melrose she had been meeting secretly. His rage, he knew, was not for Aubrey, who had been betrayed, but for himself. That realization merely intensified his anger.

"And why did he bring it to you secretly?" demanded Barrisford. "And why did you say nothing to Aubrey, who went to Liverpool in search of that very ring?"

She was silent for a moment. "I knew nothing of why Aubrey went to Liverpool," she responded quietly, "but even if I had known, I would not have felt that this is a trouble he should have to deal with. He has inherited enough problems with my father's estate. Julian and I were going to investigate this ourselves. And, after all," she added defensively, "it will make no difference to my father. It will not bring him back."

She felt distinctly underhanded as she said this, for she knew her father was snugly tucked away in an out-of-the-way cottage on Julian's property, and that he would soon be reappearing, after she was safely married to Aubrey. Julian had been horrified when his bailiff had arrived home from his journey and told his master what he had seen. Julian had posted him back with the money to reclaim the ring, and Caxton had arrived last night with it.

"What were you going to do with the ring?"

he demanded harshly. "Sell it and pocket the profit?" He took her roughly in his arms. "Did you and Julian plot your father's murder?"

Startled by his first question and enraged by the other two, Rosemary tore herself free and skated rapidly back toward the Hall. Barrisford, taken by surprise, tried for a moment to catch her, but he could see that it was useless. She was as light as thistledown moving across the ice. Frustrated, he returned slowly to his room, the ring still in his pocket.

In her own room, Rosemary stood with her hot cheek pressed against the icy windowpane, watching him slowly cross the snow-covered expanse of lawn between the lake and the Hall. Despite herself, she could not dismiss the memory of his embrace—the strength of his arms, the fierce pressure of his lips, the piercing hint of lime that lingered on his clothing remained as sharply real to her as though she were experiencing them still. For a moment she closed her eyes and gave herself freely to the memory; then, remembering her situation, she shook herself abruptly and turned from the window. He was a despicable man, she reminded herself, and she wondered if he would go directly to Aubrey and tell him his suspicions. The thought made her nervous for a moment, until she remembered Barrisford's own remark about Aubrey's new firmness. He would not give way to his uncle's pressure

She was fortunate indeed that she was marrying Aubrey. She could not imagine what it would be like to be married to a man such as Barrisford. Even though there was no passion in her relationship with Aubrey, at least she would be comfortable.

And Barrisford meant nothing to her.

Eleven

It was Christmas Eve, and Rosemary was quite determined that, Barrisford or no Barrisford, ring or no ring, it was going to be an enjoyable evening for everyone. Mrs. O'Ryan and the cousins had been bustling about the kitchen all day, she and Julian and Anne had taken the children out to collect the rest of the greenery for decorating, and the children had come home and worked with a will.

The result that evening was delightful. In the glow of candlelight and firelight, the great hall and drawing room and dining room all softened by their dressings of green and festive red ribbon, it was scarcely noticeable that the draperies were worn or the upholstery on the sofas growing threadbare. Even family portraits were wreathed in holly and ivy, and Barrisford discovered when he repaired to his bedchamber that it, too, had undergone a transformation. With great ceremony Julian and Robert and John had dragged in the largest log that they had been able to locate and carry, and had lighted it in the cavernous fireplace of the great hall. Altogether it was agreed when they met for dinner that the children had done a remarkable job of giving the house the proper Christmas spirit.

They were joined after dinner that evening by some of the families that Aubrey had met earlier: the Carters, the Haverfords, and Colonel Forester. The Carters had two young boys and a son the age of Isabella, the Haverfords a young daughter and a son home from Oxford, and Colonel Forester his two young grandsons. Barrisford watched in amusement as the great hall, large as it was, seemed to fill to overflowing with children.

Some of the older people had settled down to a serious game of cards, but the younger ones were looking for livelier amusements. Soon the hall echoed with cries of "Snip! Snap! Dragon!" punctuated by occasional wails of pain as a hand lingered too long in the bowl. Mrs. O'Ryan had set the brandy aflame in the bowl and tossed in the requisite handful of raisins.

"Go ahead, Robert!" John urged. "Just be quick about it and pop them in your mouth and close it immediately. That will put out the flame."

Robert, who had been lingering dubiously at the edge of the crowd, watching some of the others snatch back scorched fingers, edged closer to the bowl.

"See, it's easy! Just like this!" And John snaked his hand into the flames, snatched two of the raisins, and tossed them into his mouth, closing it immediately.

Thus encouraged, Robert prepared for his dive, while the others chorused:

With his blue and lapping tongue
Many of you will be stung,
        Snip! Snap! Dragon!

Finally, he dove for one of the raisins at the edge, imitating his brother's snakelike movement. Triumphantly he jerked his prize from the brandy and put it in his mouth immediately, snapping it shut.

"You see, Robert, you can do it!" exclaimed John. "Want to have another go at it?"

Robert shook his head. Once had been enough. He knew now that he could do it, but he saw no reason to trust to luck again.

"Let's play blindman's buff," he suggested, hoping to divert attention to another sport.

There was a general cry of approval, and Anne departed in search of a blindfold. By the time she had returned with a black silk handkerchief, Richard Carter had been chosen as the blindman. Anne tied the kerchief securely, reminding him severely that there must be no peeping, and the rest of the group scattered. Barrisford was firmly of the opinion that young Mr. Carter could see quite clearly, for not only did he corner a group of small ones into a screaming mass in the corner, but, having done so, he turned without touching one of them and made straight for Lady Anne and caught her around the waist. When reproved for not playing fairly, he protested vigorously and offered to be the blindman again, just to prove it. Anne, having recovered her composure and rearranged her dress, denied him the privilege and took the handkerchief herself.

The merriment was great when she caught Colonel Forester, who wasn't even playing and looked somewhat startled to have his shoulder suddenly clutched as he was talking to Cousin Matilda. Barrisford found that he was enjoying the occasion much more than he had anticipated, not because he was joining in the fun, but because everyone seemed so happy—and because he could stand here and watch Lady Rosemary with no one, least of all that lady, suspecting what he was about.

She was wearing a gown of green velvet, banded in gold, and wore ribbons of the same green in her dark tumbled curls. She had joined actively in the game of blindman's buff, and it appeared to him that both Aubrey and Julian stayed rather closer to her than was necessary. When Anne swung her arms in their direction, Rosemary had jumped back, only to find both gentlemen right behind her, and the three of them tumbled into an undignified heap on the sofa behind them, much to the amusement of the younger set.

He knew that the ring must be weighing heavily on her mind, yet she acted now as though she did not have a care in the world. Long practice, more than likely, he decided after thinking it over. Undoubtedly her father's behavior and her position of responsibility here had given her more than one anxious moment that she had had to conceal from the world. He could almost admire her insouciance if it did not directly affect Aubrey—and, he admitted to himself reluctantly, if she were engaged to him instead of Aubrey. It was an unusual feeling to know that, for the first time since his youthful disaster, he wished to spend the rest of his life with someone—and she was a fortune hunter and, perhaps, even an accessory to murder.

Still, she was undeniably lovely. Julian was now the blindman and it appeared that he could see quite as well as young Mr. Carter had been able to, and he presently had Anne and Rosemary fairly caught. Aubrey was watching the merriment a little wistfully, and Isabella had come over to take his hand.

"You mustn't mind, Aubrey. They are always like that," she said gently. "You must remember that they were all children together."

"So were you, Bella," he said sadly. "And

yet you are not out there with them." He had fallen into the habit of using the family's name for her. She was a soft-spoken, gentle girl, he reflected, and frail of course. She should be taken better care of. It was one of the things he intended to see to after his marriage to Rosemary.

"Yes, but I have never had the same lively disposition," she returned. "Rosemary and Anne are very spirited, and Rosemary rarely has an opportunity to show it. She must spend all of her time looking after the family." She smiled and patted his hand. "So don't begrudge her a little fun."

He smiled back at her, thinking how understanding she was for one so young. "I don't, Bella. And doesn't she look lovely in her gown?" he asked proudly. Then he added hurriedly, "So all of you do. You look radiant tonight."

"It was very generous of you to order these for us, Aubrey." She hesitated a moment. "Although I feel a little guilty not wearing black for Father."

"You need not," he said firmly. "After all, these gowns were ordered at my request, and I wanted you to have some cheerful things. Whether it is proper or not, you have gone too long in your old frocks for the new ones to be made up in black. If you insist, after the wedding we will have mourning clothes made. It could be considered bad luck to wear black while preparing for a wedding, you know," he added.

She looked shocked. "We wouldn't want to do anything that would make your wedding day less than happy, Aubrey. Of course we will wait."

He smiled with satisfaction. It was a pleasure to help someone like Bella, who looked to him for advice and assistance. He was not certain that Rosemary felt precisely that way about his help, however. Although she had said nothing, he sometimes had the impression that she preferred to handle matters herself, and he wanted to feel that she leaned on him.

Barrisford slipped out of the crowd and made his way to the drawing room, where he let himself out upon the snow-covered terrace. After a few moments he heard the door open behind him.

"Are you quite well, Lord Barrisford?" inquired Rosemary.

Surprised, he turned to face her. "Very well, thank you, Lady Rosemary. I just needed a few moments of peace and quiet." He studied her face for a moment. "It was very kind of you to look after me," he added.

She smiled brightly, having resolved to act as though nothing had happened. "It was no trouble, my lord," she replied briskly. "After all, you will soon be my uncle as well as Aubrey's, and it wouldn't do to have you unhappy or ill."

His gray eyes grew colder at her words. "Of course, how very thoughtful of you. I had forgotten that I shall be your uncle. How delightful that would be."

"Will be, my lord," she corrected him gently. "I'm sure that Aubrey would be very interested to know just how delightful you feel it would be."

Rosemary had decided that she would be very bright and cheerful, quite an ordinary hostess, with her unmannerly guest. After all, she could not tell Aubrey about Barrisford's behavior without causing him pain. She had glossed over unpleasant situations before, she told herself; this was just one more.

She did wish, though, that he had not come. He had quite cut up her peace of mind. Despite his roughness and his infuriating way of assuming the worst about her, she could not put him completely from her mind. He had taken her in his arms twice that day, neither time in affection, yet she could close her eyes and feel his nearness again. Aubrey's embraces did not have the same effect at all.

Barrisford watched her, wondering what she was thinking. "What has kept you from telling Aubrey about my unwelcome advances?" he asked. "He would have believed you and been extremely angry with me. In fact, he probably would have asked me to leave."

"I think that you have answered your own question, my lord," she responded gently.

"Why would I wish to cause him additional pain? He is very fond of you."

She had turned to let herself back into the drawing room. "Although I must say that I think he is misguided, I do not wish to be the cause of his unhappiness," she said briskly. "Nor do I wish for you to catch your death of cold, for then you would have to stay on instead of leaving after our wedding."

He smiled and, for a moment, looked almost approachable. "Then by all means I must come in, Lady Rosemary. On no account would I wish to inconvenience you. I had not considered that aspect of the matter."

He held the door open for her, standing uncomfortably close as she passed by him. Still, she managed a cool smile as she rejoined the others. Several of them had gathered in the music room for dancing, and Cousin Matilda had taken her place at the piano. Barrisford danced only once that evening, and that with Lady Isabella, leading her out with a smile. Rosemary noticed his action with approval, thinking that she could truly like the man if he treated everyone as he treated Bella.

When the last of the guests had gone, and the children were finally tucked in bed and settled for the night, Rosemary went downstairs once again to inspect the rooms and extinguish the candles. She paused to enjoy the beauty of the Hall in its Christmas trimmings before putting out the last of them. The snow was falling softly now, and she went to the window to watch it gathering on the sill. As she turned away from the bright stillness, the Hall seemed darker than ever, most of it lost in shadow. Only the fading golden glow of the fire provided a gentle wash of light.

"Do you never sleep, Lady Rosemary?" inquired a voice that did indeed sound very sleepy.

Having thought herself alone, Rosemary paused for a moment to gather her nerves. "I was just about to go up to bed, my lord," she replied. "I was not aware that you were still here," she added tartly.

He chuckled. "No, I realize you did not. I had changed and gone out to the stable to check my gelding's leg. Did I startle you?"

"Of course not. My heart always races like this."

He had risen from his place in the shadows, and he moved closer to her as she spoke.

"Does it indeed?" he inquired gently. "That doesn't sound at all healthy, Lady Rosemary." And reaching out, he had taken her wrist in his hand and was taking her pulse.

"That really is not necessary, my lord, as you are well aware—" she began, but he silenced her. "I can't take your pulse properly if you are speaking," he said.

He released her wrist and placed his fingers gently at the base of her throat. "I can take it more readily like this, my lady. It would never do for you to fall ill when so many depend upon you."

She opened her mouth to speak, but he put a finger over her lips, and she subsided. She was keenly aware of the gentle pressure of his fingers and the intent way in which he was studying her. She did not meet his eyes until a minute had passed and he suddenly cupped his hand beneath her chin and lifted it.

"Look above you, Lady Rosemary," he whispered.

They were once more under the kissing bough, and seeing that, she felt her knees beginning to grow weak, for his intentions were evident. Folding her close to him, he again pressed his lips against hers, this time with a firm but gentle kiss. The faint scent of lime clung to him, and she knew suddenly that for the rest of her life, whenever she encountered that fragrance, she would remember this moment. Without her willing it, her arms slipped around his neck and she responded with all the ardor of a newly awakened passion.

The strength of her reaction shook him, both by its sincerity and its innocence, and he cursed himself. For so many years he had carefully stayed away from vulnerable, inexperienced young women, and spent his time with women who knew how to play the game. Now he had done what he had meticulously avoided—and the young woman was Aubrey's fiancée.

He pulled himself abruptly away, and she looked up at him, puzzled. She had recognized the power of his emotion, and she had not thought that he could break off so suddenly.

"Is there something wrong?" she asked slowly.

"No, no of course not, my lady. How should there be anything wrong?" he asked bitterly. "I must beg your pardon. I forgot for the moment that—"

Anger and humiliation surged through her. "You forgot that I am betrothed to your nephew? Or was it that you forgot that you suspect me of murdering my father? It must be a terrible blow to your pride to find yourself attracted to a murderess!"

Taking her candle from the table, she turned and fled up the stairs, leaving Barrisford alone with the firelight, the snow, and his thoughts.

Twelve

On Christmas Day the family arose early and rode through the frosty morning to the church in the village. Like the Hall, it, too, had been decorated with greens, except that within the holy confines of the church no mistletoe was allowed, for it was considered an unholy plant, having been used long ago by the Druids for their pagan rites. It was clear that the Trevelyan family were in the habit of attending the church, for the children knew exactly what to do.

They settled themselves seriously with Julian in his pew so that there would be enough room for all the adults in the Trevelyan family pew. The service was simple, but Barrisford found it difficult to pay strict attention to the efforts of the parson and the choir and the organist. He could see several monuments belonging to the Trevelyans, and he wondered if, several years from now, Aubrey and Rosemary would be seated in this same pew together,

175

their own children ranged beside them. Perhaps he and Amelia would be seated here as well—although he had some difficulty picturing Amelia doing so gracefully—and he would be the aging bachelor uncle, spending Christmas with the family. It was a bleak prospect, and he felt again how unbearable it would be to sit by and know Rosemary only as a member of the family.

When they left the church, most of the village had gathered in the churchyard to pay their respects to Lady Rosemary and the new duke. It was clear to Barrisford that she was held in great affection and respect, and that they had heard rumors of the coming marriage and approved it. And why should they not, he thought, looking at the happy couple. Aubrey is the new duke, he is handsome, he is amiable—and he has been spending with a free hand in the village. He dismissed the last thought as unworthy, but he was certain that it had done Aubrey no disservice in the eyes of the tradesmen.

The Christmas dinner that followed made it clear that Mrs. O'Ryan had been busily taking advantage of the accounts Aubrey had opened for her in the village. Although there was no boar's head with a lemon in its mouth and sprigs of rosemary decorating it, the goose and sirloin of beef and mince pie more than atoned for its absence. The food was simple, but well prepared, and, abstemious in his habits though he was, Barrisford allowed Isabella and Candace to press him into sampling everything on the board.

Nor had he planned to partake of the plum pudding, but when Mrs. O'Ryan entered, carrying it on a large silver tray handsomely wreathed with holly, he again allowed himself to be persuaded.

"Be careful when you bite down, my lord," advised Candace, "or you might break a tooth on one of the tokens."

Thus adjured, Barrisford chewed carefully. There was a great deal of laughter when Rosemary found a coin in her portion, a portent which promised that she would become wealthy during the following year.

"Very soon in the year—on New Year's Day to be exact," laughed Aubrey. "Then everything I have will be yours, too, my dear." At his words Rosemary's eyes flew to Lord Barrisford, certain that he would be angered by this blatant referral to her marrying for money, but he merely looked at her enigmatically. It was left to Uncle Webster to propose a toast to the happy couple, and they all drank to them cheerfully, even Barrisford raising his glass with at least the appearance of approval.

"There is no better day for my wedding than New Year's," said Aubrey, "for it will be the beginning of a whole new life for me—for both of us." He added the last bit swiftly, having perceived in Rosemary's eye her reaction

177

to the "me," as though he were the only one who would be changed by the marriage.

To his surprise, Barrisford found that he, too, had a token in his pudding, and he carefully extracted a small gold ring.

"You're to be married this year, my lord!" crowed Will. "You must keep that for the wedding ring!"

There was a startled pause, and then, after a glimpse at Barrisford's face, Aubrey raised his glass high. "It is more than time, Uncle. You have kept the ladies waiting long enough," he said, chuckling. "I shall be delighted to see you caught in the parson's mousetrap at last. And rest assured that we shall dance at your wedding."

The laughter became general, and, despite himself, Barrisford glanced at Rosemary, who turned swiftly toward Julian on her left.

After dinner followed a noisy game of forfeits, and Isabella would not allow Barrisford to retire to the sidelines to watch.

"You spend too much time to one side, Lord Barrisford," she said reproachfully. "And we do need everyone for the game—won't you join us?"

Had it been anyone else, he could easily have declined, but he would have felt churlish to refuse the gentle Isabella. Reluctantly he took his place among the others. John was the Crier of the Forfeits, taking great joy in deciding the penalties that must be paid. Uncle

Webster was forced to give up his pipe for an hour; Rosemary forfeited one of her green velvet ribbons; Will, who hated to sing, was forced to stand alone and sing "Good King Wencelas" for the company; Anne was made to kiss Julian. Several members of the company had offered to depose Master Will and allow him a taste of his own medicine, but fortunately for him there was a sudden diversion when company arrived at the door.

Outside stood a Christmas choir, complete with small orchestra, and the strains of "God Rest You Merry Gentlemen" sounded sweetly—for the most part—through the gently falling snow. Mr. Tipton's baritone was consistently off-key and someone amongst the sopranos had decided to warble a bit more than necessary, but the overall effect was charming. The Trevelyans and their guests gathered at the door and at the windows and listened with pleasure as the choir continued with "The First Noel" and "While Shepherds Watched."

Barrisford stood well back from the others. Listening to the choir was a simple pleasure and many of his friends in London would have lifted their noses at the lack of sophistication on the part of the singers; still, he almost wished that his life had included an honest enjoyment of experiences such as this. He enjoyed rural pleasures in faraway countries, where they somehow seemed more exotic, but at home in England they had simply seemed provincial.

Matilda was also standing a little apart from the others, and after a moment he noticed that she was pressing a small wisp of handkerchief to her eyes.

"Are you all right, Miss Trevelyan?" he inquired gently.

Having not realized that anyone had observed her, she became a little more flurried than usual. "Oh yes, my lord, so very kind of you to notice. I am quite all right."

"Are you, perhaps, remembering other Christmases?" His voice remained gentle, for it was not in his manner to treat unkindly those who were beneath him in station.

She looked up at him gratefully, dabbing at her faded blue eyes. Indeed, everything about Cousin Matilda—and her sister, of course—seemed a little faded: cheeks that were faintly pink, chestnut hair drained of its color and threaded with gray, even the little lockets at their throats were no longer brightly golden.

"Yes, my lord, that is a part of it, of course—remembering poor Mama and Papa—and Raymond, of course."

"Was Raymond your husband?" he inquired politely.

"Oh, no!" she fluttered. "Raymond was our brother." Here she dabbed at her eyes again. "And he took such wonderful care of us until his death last spring."

Barrisford tried to look reasonably interested, but he was tiring rapidly. He devoutly
hoped that he was not going to be subjected
to a homily on Raymond's virtues. Nonetheless, he managed to look properly interested
and to murmur his condolences.

"Yes, he was a great loss because we had
always loved dear Raymond so—and we had
stayed close even after he married and had a
family of his own. And, of course, he always
took care of us. Mama and Papa's money went
to Raymond when they died because they knew
that he would manage it well and look after
us. And he always did. We always went there
at Christmas and had such a lovely time—why
we had carolers there just like this last Christmas."

"I am certain that you miss him—and his
family," returned Barrisford politely. "Do you
live close to them?"

"We used to," replied Matilda hesitantly.
"But that was when Raymond was alive and
taking care of things for us. We had a charming little cottage just half a mile down the
road from them. It had the dearest garden."

As she looked up, her twin beckoned to her
from her position close to the door, and she
excused herself to Barrisford and hurried over.
Isabella had been standing next to them during the last part of Matilda's reply, and she
turned to Barrisford after Matilda was out of
hearing.

"They had a cottage until Raymond died, and his wife took everything," she said sharply. Barrisford was unaccustomed to hearing such a tone in Isabella's voice, and he looked at her curiously. "Since their brother hadn't specifically provided for them in his will, his wife informed them that there simply wasn't enough money for her to be able to continue their upkeep in the cottage and take care of the children, too."

"And they came here?" he asked.

"And they came here," she replied. "And of course Rosemary wouldn't turn them away. And so now they consider this their home—but I know they still miss their cottage." She smiled. "Rosemary said once that if our ship ever came in, we would buy it back for them."

"And she didn't mind taking them in?" he asked curiously.

Isabella looked shocked. "No, of course not, my lord. After all, they are family, and where else would they go? There aren't any provisions made for people like them."

Their conversation slowed as the choristers began their last carol, the "Wassail Song."

Love and joy come to you,
And to you your wassail too,
And God bless you, and send you
A happy New Year,
And God send you a happy New Year.

182

When the last words had died away, Rosemary opened wide the front door and invited them all in. Together they streamed into the great hall and Mrs. O'Ryan came in with a bowl of steaming wassail, fragrant with nutmeg and ginger and steaming crab apples.

Healths were drunk and the crowd grew very merry, particularly when they toasted "Lord Stedham and his new lady," saying "Health and long life to them." The cheers were loud, and thus encouraged, Aubrey kissed his bride-to-be under the mistletoe, again winning the applause of the crowd. Barrisford reflected that Amelia would have deplored the lack of propriety, but he could not feel so supercilious. That their affection for Lady Rosemary was real he had no doubt, and he was beginning to feel again that Aubrey was getting the best of the bargain in their marriage. Fortune hunters did not as a rule take in poverty-stricken family members and make them feel as though they belonged.

In the general commotion, Barrisford stopped beside the table on which lay Rosemary's velvet ribbon from the game of forfeits. Glancing about to be certain that no one was watching, he slipped it into a pocket of his waistcoat, next to the ring. Now he must decide what to do next. He was determined that Aubrey would not marry Lady Rosemary, not because he wished to remove him from the dangers of Marston Hall, but because he wished to marry her himself. Whether she was a fortune hunter, a saint, or a murderess—he intended to marry her.

Thirteen

Rosemary awoke the next morning in a bleak mood, and she lay for a moment wondering what could have caused it. Then it all came rushing back to her: Lord Barrisford. If he would only take himself away, she might be able to go on with her plans to save Marston Hall and the family without any second thoughts. She had determined that she would accept Aubrey, for she had seen no other possible choice. Barrisford had offered her money, of course, to refuse to marry Aubrey, but there was no assurance in that—nor would she stoop to blackmail.

A fine distinction to make, she thought ruefully, forcing herself to get up and face the day. She would be marrying him under false pretenses at any rate. Still, as she had told herself when he first approached her, she was making a bargain that she would keep with her promise of marriage; she would have no trouble being a good wife, for Aubrey was a kind and worthy man. She would see to it that he did not suffer through their partnership. It was the least she could do. She thought dismally, however, that she would make a much better wife to Aubrey if his uncle decided to reside in China for the foreseeable future.

She dressed in front of a crackling fire, an unaccustomed luxury that Aubrey had provided for them. He had declared that there would be no more icy bedrooms. There was no more need to be careful about the amount of fuel used because he would now be providing for them. She sighed as she pulled on her stockings—if only he weren't quite so determined to take care of them, she thought. Then she laughed—why else was she marrying him if not so that he would provide for them? She must remember to be grateful and to stop trying to give him advice about how things should be done. After all, he thought himself to be the owner of the Hall, and he was most certainly the one spending the money. It was simply that she disliked handing over the reins after controlling things for so many years. It would take some readjustment on her part.

And then there was the ever-lurking Barrisford. When he had asked her why she hadn't told Aubrey about his "unwelcome advances," she had told him only part of the truth. She did not, naturally, wish to cause Aubrey pain, but that was only a part of it. She had been wondering if Barrisford was not trying to entrap her. It had occurred to her that he might wish to tell Aubrey that she had succumbed to his advances. It would be exactly the kind of behavior Barrisford would expect of her. And Aubrey would doubtless be horrified and break off the engagement.

She shivered for a moment, despite the fire, as she remembered what it had felt like to be in his arms last night—and how she very nearly had given way to her traitorous emotions. It was hard to say whether she was more angry with herself or with him—but she did wonder why he had broken off. Her behavior last night would have offered him the golden opportunity to carry tales to Aubrey. Heaven only knew how she would have behaved if he had not called a halt to things.

The gown that she slipped into, grateful for its warmth, was one of the new ones Aubrey had ordered for her, a deep crimson one made of fine woolen cloth. She swept up her knot of dusky curls and fixed them in place with a pair of combs of antique gold that had belonged to her mother. Glancing in the glass, she smiled at her reflection. "That's it," she said. "You need to remember to smile and look happy. After all, you're about to be married, my girl." Then, praying that she would not find Barrisford in the dining room at this early hour, she descended.

It was a prayer not to be granted, however. Barrisford was very much there, eating his toast placidly and reading a three-day-old paper. He looked up at her and raised an eyebrow.

"You are up very early this morning, Lady Rosemary," he observed, quite as though he himself were accustomed to arising shortly after dawn.

"I don't know how you could be aware of whether this is earlier than usual or not, my lord. I don't recall seeing you abroad at this hour." She felt that at this point in their relationship, she could dispense with any of the pleasant small talk a hostess is normally supposed to make.

"I simply supposed that, since you keep such late hours—skating and wandering about downstairs in the darkness—that you must need your rest in the morning, Lady Rosemary." And he went calmly back to his toast, ignoring the indignant glance she gave him.

Rosemary was seething, but she could not think of anything she could say to him that would not reflect upon herself. How dare he bring up those two unhappy episodes and act as though he had nothing to do with either one of them!

Finally she managed to say in her usual pleasant tone, pouring her tea as nonchalantly as though she were discussing the weather, "It would seem to me that you might be tired for the same reasons, my lord."

Without glancing up from his paper, he replied in a brisk voice, "No, indeed, Lady Rosemary. I found the experiences most—invigorating." He paused over the last word for a moment, as though it gave him pleasure to say it.

"I expect that you would find them so, my lord," she returned sweetly, determined upon vengeance against this arrogant, annoying man. "I am sure that seizing a kiss under the mistletoe is an elevating experience for someone who has no hope of a kiss that is freely given."

He lowered the newspaper briefly and his eyes met hers coolly. "You are quite mistaken about that, Lady Rosemary. I am sure that the same thing would have happened had there been no kissing bough. And I am equally sure that it will happen again."

Rosemary's fingers ached to close around the heavy silver candlestick just in front of her. She longed to heave it at him and see him fold slowly to the floor so that he would harass her no longer. The arrogance of the man! He thought that he had merely to come close to her and all her defenses would collapse. She ignored the reasonable portion of her mind, which was pointing out that that was precisely what had happened. She simply wished to see that small smile, so nearly a smirk, wiped from his face. Her fingers edged toward the candlestick.

"I wouldn't try it, you know," he said conversationally. "You will miss and probably break something—and how will you explain such behavior on your part to the others? I believe that they expect more of you, Lady Rosemary."

And he retired behind his papers again, apparently quite certain that she would do nothing. And of course that is precisely what she did—nothing. She was shocked that she, usually so even-tempered and pleasant, could be moved to such an urge for violence. For a moment she thought it would be well worth it just to see the expression on his face should she do it—and hit her mark. Then, however, she remembered all of the others to whom she was responsible and how she would deplore any such act on their part. Moreover, she decided, she would not give him the pleasure of seeing her lose her temper—no matter how tempting he made it.

"I do hope, Uncle Robert," she began sweetly, then stopped abruptly as though doubtful. "You don't mind my calling you so, do you? I have heard so much from Aubrey that I do feel as though you really were my uncle."

He looked at her suspiciously. "I see no need for you to do so, Lady Rosemary," he said haughtily. "After all, at the moment the relationship between us really doesn't exist." And he attempted to retire behind his papers.

Having found a sore spot, Rosemary pursued her point with relish. "Oh, I understand what must be bothering you, my lord. *Do* forgive me for not thinking of it."

He lowered the paper suspiciously, just enough to allow him to look over the top. "For not thinking of what?"

"Why, of *it,* of course, just as I said. Since you are so certain that *it* will happen again, I'm sure it would make you feel uneasy to hear me calling you 'Uncle Robert' at such a time."

He retired behind the paper again, but she noticed with satisfaction that it was fairly twitching with annoyance. As she rose to excuse herself from the table, she strolled behind his chair and whispered in his ear.

"So pray don't give *it* another thought, my lord. I'm sure that your nephew would applaud your careful observation of the proprieties."

Before she could depart after this home shot, the door to the dining room opened and Matilda appeared, wearing a worried expression. "A note came for you, Rose," she announced, waving a carefully folded paper in her direction. "I can't imagine who it could be from, though."

Barrisford's attention was captured by this, and he watched covertly as she unfolded it. His immediate thought was that Julian was the author, and he wondered if they had an assignation. He noted that her cheeks flamed as she read it; then she carefully folded it up again and put it in the pocket of her gown. She turned and left the room without saying anything to either Barrisford or Matilda, both of whom stared after her.

"I do hope that it wasn't bad news," fluttered Matilda. "I must go and see if I can offer any help." Then, remembering Rosemary's abandoned duties as hostess, she turned and asked hopefully, "Is there anything that I could get for you, Lord Barrisford?"

He shook his head. "Thank you, Miss Trevelyan. I have everything that I need." The instant that the door closed behind her, Barrisford was on his feet, prepared to follow her upstairs as soon as he inconspicuously could. Once there, he slipped into a chamber not presently in use and left the door open a crack so that he would see if Lady Rosemary left her room. He had no intention of her leaving the house without his knowing her destination.

Once Rosemary had reached the safety of her own room, she pulled out the note she had received and read it again. Its author was obviously not well educated, for the handwriting was uneven and many of the words misspelled. Still, the writer had managed to convey his threat. He knew of her father's plan and threatened to expose them to Aubrey

Townsend if she did not meet him that morning at a nearby inn with a substantial payment for his silence. And it was signed "A Friend from the *Lovely Lady*."

Rosemary was frantic. She had very little ready cash herself, and she knew that Julian, who was the only one she could call upon, normally did not keep much at home either. How very like her father to do business with someone who would turn about and blackmail him! And the letter had left her with little doubt that the letter's author would not hesitate to go directly to Aubrey in the hope of receiving some financial reward from him if she failed to appear that morning.

She opened her jewelry case and stared into it. There was nothing there but trinkets. Aside from her pearls, the only thing of value that she possessed was the sapphire set left to her by her mother, and she did not wish to part with it. Nonetheless, she took the velvet case with her, slipping it under her cloak. She had changed into her riding habit and was ready to ride to Melrose Manor and collect Julian to face the blackmailer with her.

As luck would have it, Julian had ridden out earlier in the morning, and his time of return was uncertain. There was no choice then, she decided, scribbling a note and leaving it with the housekeeper. She would have to go alone. After all, the Swan, where the man was staying, was a respectable inn, although small and out of the way. Although it certainly wasn't the proper thing for her to be doing, she could surely come to no harm. And what was more to the point, she thought, clutching her sapphires, her jewels could come to no harm.

She was less certain of this when she found herself closeted in a tiny private parlor with a man of massive proportions and grim expression.

"Did you bring me somethin' then, my fine lady?" he asked with a leer that revealed three ominous-looking gold teeth as he stretched out his hand.

"I would like to hear just what you know first," she responded coolly, clutching the sapphires firmly under her cloak.

"I know everything there is to know," he said with a wink. "I know that your papa paid to have the captain of the *Lovely Lady* report to a Mr. Crispin in London that he had gone overboard—and then we set him down quietly when we made port in Liverpool. And I know that in the meantime there's a brand-new duke in your papa's place, one who's got the dibs in tune. Now then—" And he again stretched out his hand.

"You must understand that I do not have a great deal of ready cash," she heard herself saying, wondering how she could bargain with him to guarantee that payment this time would keep him away. Soon, of course, it would all be out in the open and this man could do no harm, but in the meantime, it was undoubtedly dangerous to leave him strolling about, ready to tell his tale to anyone who would listen.

Before she could say anything, however, the door flew open and Julian entered hurriedly. "Rose, whatever are you doing here alone?" he exclaimed.

"This here's a private meetin' betwixt me and the lady!" protested the hulk towering over them in the middle of the tiny room.

"You forget yourself, sir," said Julian, turning a cool eye upon him. "A proper young lady would never meet a man—particularly one such as yourself—alone. I believe there was a misunderstanding. She had intended to wait for my arrival before joining you."

"Well, you're here now," announced the man. "Best make my settlement before I have to head toward Marston Hall with some news for the new duke—that he *isn't* the new duke."

"You know, Julian, that we have to do this," she said in a low voice.

Julian looked the man over one more time, as though speculating on his possibility of succeeding if he launched himself at the fellow with no warning. He correctly judged, however, that his size precluded any such move. From all indications, he had been drinking heavily too, even though it was early morning—and his clothes smelled of alcohol.

Julian took a small roll of bills from his

pocket and handed it to the stranger. "Here take this, fellow, and then take yourself as far away from here as it is possible to go."

The man growled as he counted out the bills. "Not enough!" he exclaimed, throwing them down on the table. "Don't you know my news is worth more than this? You'll have to do better than this to keep me from the new duke."

Julian looked a little disconcerted at this remark, but he was horrified when Rosemary held out a large velvet case to him. "It's the sapphires, Julian," she said in a low voice. "They were all I could think of."

"No, Rosemary, you most certainly will not give them to this fellow!" he said emphatically, ignoring the darkening look on the man's face. He handed the case back to her.

The man started to snatch for it, but Julian brought down his riding crop across the top of his hand, causing him to jerk back in pain.

"You will leave the lady's jewels alone, sir," he said angrily. "You have no right to them."

"We'll see about that," he muttered. "What am I to get then?"

"The money that I gave you, my man, and that is more than enough for the likes of you."

"Let me have them combs," he said, eyeing Rosemary's hair greedily. "Let me have them combs, I say, and with those and the money I'll engage to keep myself out of your way."

"Very well," Julian replied grimly, "although

I hate to make a deal with any man of your stamp."

The man, taking this as a backhand compliment, chuckled. "You're wise to do so, sir. Not all of them who do business with me live to tell the tale."

Julian handed him the roll of bills and the combs, while Rosemary tried to tidy her disarranged hair as best she could. She was not looking forward to walking out through the public room looking as she did, but there was little choice in the matter. Still carefully carrying the case, she made her way down the stairs with Julian in her wake. Close behind them came their nemesis, the man mountain, chuckling in satisfaction.

Barrisford sat alone in the farthest corner of the public room, as carefully screened from view as possible. As the three of them made their way down the stairs, his eyes widened in surprise. Despite all of the things he had thought about Lady Rosemary, he had never really believed that she might be capable of such a thing as this. She was obviously not the innocent everyone took her to be. As he took them in at a glance, he noted her disheveled appearance, the disreputable look of the stranger with her, and the proprietary air of Julian as he guided her down the steps.

When they had left, he did not follow them immediately. He made a few inquiries at the bar about the man with them, but he learned very little of consequence about the stranger. He was a sailor, he had little money, he had come Christmas night and had demanded a private parlor for a meeting the next morning.

As he rode slowly home, he made his plans, blotting from his mind the lovely disarray of Lady Rosemary's hair and any thought of how it had come to be disarranged. Instead, he thought of Aubrey. He would watch his nephew carefully, and at all costs he would stop the wedding. It was the only way to save his nephew.

Fourteen

Before he arrived back at Marston Hall, Barrisford encountered Aubrey and Lady Isabella walking in the park. He reined in and looked at them in surprise. Lady Isabella's cheeks were surprisingly pink and her eyes were merry; she seemed almost to glow. Aubrey had taken her arm protectively and together they were making away along the edge of the drive.

"Isn't it too cold for you to be out, Lady Isabella?" he inquired, thinking of what her sister had told him about her fragility.

"No, not at all, my lord," she replied. "Or at least it isn't too cold if I am out only for a while."

"We decided that she needed more fresh air than she had been getting since the weather grew wintry," explained Aubrey seriously. "It seemed to me that it would be much better for her to get a little fresh air and exercise each day than to sit all of the time in the Hall, breathing in the smoke of the fires."

Barrisford tipped his hat to them. "It sounds wise to me, but more to the point, Lady Isabella, you look in greater health than any day since I arrived."

"It is all your nephew's doing," she said, smiling. "He is so interested in the welfare of each of us."

"Indeed," smiled Barrisford, thinking that Aubrey seemed particularly interested in her welfare, more so for instance, than in that of Uncle Webster. Aubrey had the grace to blush when he caught his uncle's eye.

Unwilling to linger and perhaps encounter Julian and Rosemary, Barrisford turned his horse toward the stable. Once in the Hall, he found no sign of life until he reached the kitchen. There everyone had gathered to watch the puppies, as they had when it was the only warm room in the Hall. Annie Laurie was strolling around the kitchen, feeling more herself, but not yet lively enough to run in her usual set of circles around the perimeter of the room, leaping over all of the low obstacles in her path.

Seeing that everyone was occupied, Barrisford strolled back to the great hall, thoughtfully fingering Lady Rosemary's velvet ribbon that he had acquired on Christmas Eve. His timing was almost flawless. The door opened quietly, and his quarry let herself in without a sound, obviously hopeful that she would attract no attention. When she turned around after carefully closing the door, she saw him.

"Is that a new style?" he inquired, studying her hair critically.

Rosemary, who had hoped to reach her room unnoticed and repair the damage, tried to dismiss it lightly. "I was out riding and I lost my combs," she replied briskly. "It is such a bother, too—they belonged to my mother and I was very fond of them."

He immediately assumed an air of concern. "Then we must go in search of them, Lady Rosemary. It would be a pity to lose them." And he started toward the door with a resolute air.

She looked at him with irritation. He might be depended upon, she thought, to be where he was least needed. "No, my lord, I could not impose," she said hastily. "It is hopeless to go looking for them in this weather. And I covered too much ground in my ride to limit the search to just one area."

"Did you indeed?" he inquired with interest. "Where did you go? I went out for a ride myself this morning, and I was trying to think of a new route to take. I wish that I had known you were going out—I would have accompanied you."

Reflecting that he was determined to turn up like a bad penny and not wishing to say where she had been riding until she knew where he had been, she dismissed the subject.

"I scarcely remember where I was. I was so deep in thought that I simply gave my horse his head. That is another reason it will be so difficult to retrace my steps."

Satisfied that she had at last put him off, she turned and hurried toward the stairs. Pausing a moment at the landing, she turned to look back. He had said nothing in response to her last remark, and now he stood there staring after her, his face dark. Their eyes met for a moment, and then, as quickly as dignity would allow, she walked on to the safety of her room and closed the door behind her.

Sinking into a chair there, she covered her face with her hands. She must remember to bring her sapphires in from the barn where she had hidden them. She had not wished to be seen with the telltale flat velvet box and have to explain herself, and had decided to take a basket to the barn to retrieve it later. Doubtless, Lord Barrisford would wish to go with her, she reflected bitterly. He had not the least notion when he was not wanted—or, which was more likely—he did not care.

Rosemary did not think that the blackmailer would be satisfied with the money and the combs. Sooner or later, and probably sooner, he would want more. Julian felt that they had discouraged the man, but she was much less certain. Why should he be satisfied with the little they had given him? They had everything to lose if he appeared again, and he must surely know it.

Guilt was beginning to take its toll on her. Accustomed as she was to straight dealing, having to make up stories to conceal the truth was as unfamiliar and uncomfortable to her as suddenly finding herself attired in another woman's clothing. She was almost eager for the truth about her father to be known so that she could be freed from the weight of this charade.

Barrisford, after allowing himself and his horse a rest, paid another visit to the Swan. Scanning the public room and finding no sign of the sailor, he inquired of the landlord where he might find him.

"Got a trifle bosky," that individual replied dourly. "He wanted to sleep at that corner table, but it isn't good for custom. We carried him up to his room."

"And which room would that be?" asked Barrisford smoothly, placing a coin on the counter in front of the landlord.

"He is in no fit condition to be seen, my lord," he warned. "It will be a waste of your time." If he wondered what a man such as Barrisford wanted with one such as the drunken sailor upstairs, he concealed it carefully. The ways of the quality were strange ones, and that the grim individual before him

203

was a member of that select group he had not a doubt. Giving Barrisford instructions to the room, he pocketed his coin and went about his business.

The landlord had been accurate in his estimate of his customer's condition. He lay sprawled upon his cot, deep snores racking his heavy frame. Barrisford looked about him carefully. There, on a table close to the bed, lay a pair of golden combs—Lady Rosemary's combs. Silently he pocketed them, and after finding nothing more of interest and seeing that the sailor showed no immediate signs of revival, he rode thoughtfully back to Marston Hall.

A familiar carriage drawn up in front of the Hall prepared him for what he would find within. Bracing himself for the worst, he quietly entered the drawing room.

"My *dear* brother! Where *have* you been?" Amelia was reclining on one of the worn sofas, and Isabella was kneeling beside her, waving burnt feathers beneath her nose. "You might have found me lying here in a *coma,* were it not for this child's ministrations." Here she waved a graceful hand in Isabella's direction.

Isabella turned large, worried eyes toward Barrisford. "She seems very faint, my lord. I do think that she should be taken to bed as soon as possible and Mrs. O'Ryan will fix her a posset."

Amelia bestowed an approving glance upon

her. "I *think* that if I rest for a few minutes, I shall gather enough strength to go to my room."

"I shall go and ask Mrs. O'Ryan to fix the posset, Mrs. Townsend. Rosemary is having a fire lighted in your room right now, so you just rest for a few minutes. I shall be back directly."

As the door closed behind her, Amelia looked after her almost fondly. Few things agreed with her more than having someone recognize the seriousness of her afflictions. "Quite a *nice* child," she said condescendingly. "*Most* unlike her sister, who is a *bold*-faced chit if ever I saw one."

"You must remember, Amelia, that you are in Lady Rosemary's home now. You should not speak of her in such a manner here, even if that is what you think of her."

His sister stared at him. "*Whatever* are you talking about, Robert? This is *Aubrey's* house now. *He* is the duke of Stedham. Why should I *not* speak my mind about a young woman with *no* fortune and little claim to beauty who is trying to marry *my* son?"

"That is what you must remember, Amelia. Aubrey is still determined to marry Lady Rosemary, and you will only set his back up if you act as though you are going to call a halt to it."

"But, Robert, that is why I sent *you* up here—to *stop* this impossible marriage. I expected you back in London with Aubrey immediately. I did not think you would linger here through *Christmas*."

"And what did you think I would do, Sister? Kidnap him?" he inquired.

"If necessary, of course. *Nothing* would be too drastic if it removed him from that *harpy's* clutches. You *must* stop this marriage, Robert!"

"And that is what I intend to do," he returned calmly. "But I am not going to kidnap Aubrey to do so."

"*When* will you do so, Robert? And *how*?"

"You must leave that to me, Amelia," he replied.

"Your chamber is ready, Mrs. Townsend," announced a coolly modulated voice. "I thought that you might wish to lie down before dinner."

To his annoyance, he realized that Lady Rosemary had silently entered the room, and he wondered how much she had heard before he had noticed her presence.

"I am not certain that I will be *well* enough to come down for dinner," said Amelia in a failing voice, offended that Rosemary thought her well enough to bounce back after a nap. "The journey has taken a *very* heavy toll on my strength."

Rosemary, who had taken Amelia's measure in the moment of their meeting, responded briskly and unsympathetically. "Well, if that is the case, Mrs. Townsend, I will bring up a supper tray myself and sit with you while you dine."

At the thought of such a treat as this in store, Amelia collapsed back against the cushions and moaned gently. *"Robert!* You *must* help me upstairs. I *really* do not feel that I can do it alone."

"I would be happy to help you myself, Mrs. Townsend," said Rosemary briskly. "I think that it is very likely that a little exercise such as this is the very thing to restore you."

She was by now well aware of Amelia's antipathy for her, and she could not resist irritating her. It was gratifying to see that lady try to draw back even farther into the cushions, avoiding Rosemary's extended hand. "No, *no,* that will not do at all. *Robert!"* she said faintly. "Robert, *you* must assist me. Taft will be waiting in my chamber."

As she tottered into her room, a tall, angular woman swept down upon her, and tenderly helped her to a chair.

"I can*not* believe that you have not already removed my son from this *dreadful* place, Robert. *Nor* can I believe that he has not already sent the Trevelyans away. Why are *they* still lingering here when it is *Aubrey's* home?"

"In response to your first remark, Amelia, I would remind you that Aubrey is not a child to be 'removed' at your will or anyone else's. He must make his own decisions."

Before she could rush into speech, he

added, "As for why the Trevelyan family is still here, it would appear to me that there are two reasons. First, Aubrey is planning to marry one of them. Second, even if he were not planning to marry a member of the family, since this has been their home for generations, and since Jack Trevelyan's death was unexpected, his daughters have nowhere else to go. No gentleman would expect them to leave immediately."

"And what *of* Jack Trevelyan's death?" she demanded. *"What* did Aubrey mean in his letter? *Is* there a question of murder?"

Thinking of Julian and Rosemary's meeting with the sailor, and thinking of Trevelyan's death on the *Lovely Lady,* Barrisford replied slowly, "I don't know that we are speaking of murder precisely, Amelia."

"Precisely?" Amelia's voice rose almost to a shriek. "What do you mean, *precisely,* Robert? Do you mean that it might be *possible?* I might have *known* the Trevelyans would be involved in something as sordid as murder."

Barrisford frowned at her, indicating with a nod both the presence of Taft and the nearness of the door, closed though it was.

Amelia tossed her head. "Taft won't say a word, *will you,* Taft? I tell her *everything*—and as for those *doors,* Robert, they are so thick that no one could hear me *scream* for help if I were *positively shrieking. No* one will hear what we are saying."

"Nonetheless, Amelia, you must be more discreet."

She sniffed indignantly and settled more comfortably on her couch. Taft tucked her shawl firmly about her shoulders and settled a robe over her legs, then plumped the pillows and placed her smelling salts close at hand.

"*Besides*, Robert, from what Taft tells me, there are virtually *no* servants for her to gossip with should she wish to *lower* herself to doing so. They have *only* a housekeeper, a maid, and a *single* stablehand. Isn't that *so*, Taft?"

Taft, thus appealed to, nodded and pursed her lips. "I understand that the young ladies do a great deal of the common work themselves," she said, her disapproval manifest in every syllable she spoke.

Barrisford greatly disliked his sister's habit of discussing personal affairs with servants, and his feeling must have been evident, for Amelia said sharply, "And you *needn't* look so supercilious, Robert. I *quite* rely on Taft *and* Barron. I don't know *how* I would get along without them."

"I thought that Aubrey let Barron go," Barrisford said abruptly.

His sister shrugged. "I could not *allow* that to happen, Robert. You *know* that Barron has been an *excellent* counselor to Aubrey for *all* of these years. Aubrey merely *thinks* he has outgrown Barron. *Actually*, he needs Barron *more* than ever. And *so* I shall make plain to him."

"I think that you may be in for a surprise, Sister," he said dryly.

"Oh, *I* think not," she replied confidently. "Aubrey has tried *this* sort of thing before—"

"Getting married, do you mean?" he asked innocently, unable to resist temptation.

"Of *course* not!" she retorted sharply. "Naturally, I was *referring* to abandoning Barron. You *really* seem to have developed an *un*becoming streak of levity, Robert. You are *quite* as bad as that *terrible* Lady Rosemary, who *obviously* did not recognize the *serious* nature of my illness. I *wish* that *you* would take this whole matter seriously."

"Oh, I assure you that I do, Amelia."

"I can*not* have my *dear* boy marry that harpy."

"And I promise you that he will not."

"How can you be *ab*solutely certain of that, Robert?" she demanded.

He smiled down at her. "I intend to marry her myself."

If Barrisford had suddenly announced his intention of walking the length of England in his bare feet, his sister could not have looked more shocked.

"You *can*not be serious, Robert!" she exclaimed.

"But I am, Amelia. I assure you, I am."

"But what of *Aubrey?*" she asked. "What of *his* engagement?"

"It will soon be ended, Amelia. I shall see to that."

"But you would *not* marry into a nest of ne'er-do-wells and fortune hunters and murderers, Robert! Think of our *family*!"

"My dear sister, I am not thinking of our family. I am thinking of myself."

"But you *can't* mean that you *wish* to do so, Robert!"

He paused a moment, then smiled. "I know that it does sound strange, Amelia—but, yes, I do wish to do so."

Fifteen

Rosemary had made her journey to the stable to rescue her sapphires and she had stowed them carefully in the bottom of a rush basket and covered them with a linen napkin. She avoided the busy kitchen and, wary of the great hall now that she had encountered Barrisford in it too many times, admitted herself quietly through a side door. The passageway led past the bookroom that served as her office, and she was startled to see a tall, gray-haired man emerge from it and close the door.

"Mr. Barron, may I help you?" she asked in surprise. "Have you lost your way?"

"Not at all, Lady Rosemary," he replied smoothly, quite as though he were not a visitor greatly out of place. "Since I understand that you have taken care of the affairs of the estate, I asked Lady Isabella where you kept your office and she was gracious enough to tell me."

"And when you discovered that I was not in my office, Mr. Barron, what did you do?" Rosemary asked. She was normally a very soft-spoken person, but this man's air of consequence and his presence in her private domain grated upon her unbearably.

"It would, of course, have been more convenient had you been present," he conceded, "but I was able to find some of the things myself and to begin looking over the accounts."

Rosemary fingers were twitching and she had a sudden violent urge to swing at him with the basket she held. Unfortunately, it was too light, and she did not wish to damage her sapphires. Still, she could scarcely keep herself from stamping her foot as she spoke again.

"Am I to understand, Mr. Barron, that you had the temerity to let yourself into my office and to go through my desk without my permission?" She spoke in a restrained voice, but she felt as though she would like to scream the words at him.

He looked vaguely surprised. "Why, yes, of course. I would scarcely call it temerity, however. It would have been helpful to have you present to help me, still—"

"Mr. Barron! You are *not* to set foot in my office again! I have never locked the door, but there is a lock and you may rest assured that from this point on it will be used. If you have

213

no more regard for privacy than this, we may have to lock all of the doors."

"You seem to be laboring under a misapprehension, Lady Rosemary," he replied gently. "You do realize, do you not, that Marston Hall is no longer yours? That it is the property now of Aubrey Townsend?"

Silently calling down curses on the head of her absent father who had caused all of this, she replied through gritted teeth. "I do indeed, Mr. Barron. But it was not Aubrey Townsend I saw leaving my office. Nor, I might add, would Aubrey have gone into my private papers without asking my permission."

Barron looked indulgent. "No, of course he would not even think of asking to look at the books. He has never looked after his own affairs, you see."

"I think you underestimate him, Mr. Barron," she returned shortly, "and I know that you underestimate me. You are not to return to my office. Mr. Townsend, of course, is welcome to go over the accounts with me anytime—as he well knows."

Barron shrugged in amusement. "It will make no difference, Lady Rosemary. You see, I am quite accustomed to handling the affairs of both Mrs. Townsend and her son. Normally, I would have been here to do so immediately."

"Barron!" Aubrey's voice was sharp and both of them looked up, startled. Rosemary had never heard him speak in that tone, nor had

214

Barron. "I believe that before I left London I dismissed you."

Barron bowed slightly and smiled. "Your good mother and I agreed that you had acted without thinking, Aubrey. You know that you have always tended to—"

"You and my 'good mother' are quite out this time, Barron. I dismissed you deliberately, and if you are now in my mother's employ, then you must confine yourself to my mother's concerns. And those do not include Lady Rosemary's account books or anything else connected with the Trevelyan family or Marston Hall. Do I make myself quite clear?"

Barron, although a little paler than usual, still managed to retain his indulgent expression, just as though this were precisely the behavior he had expected and that he knew that soon Aubrey would see things his way. Bowing slightly, he turned and walked away.

"Rosemary, I offer my deepest apologies. I had no idea that he would consider doing anything so ill-advised. But I don't know why I didn't think of it. It is exactly in keeping with his treatment of me."

He looked so profoundly angry and miserable that Rosemary looked at him in amazement. "You don't mean to say, Aubrey, that that is his normal manner with you."

He nodded. "It has been, but I put a stop to it before leaving London. I had been trying to work up the courage to let him go for months."

They had stepped into her bookroom and closed the door behind them. It was no longer a chamber that would congeal the blood; instead, a fire leaped merrily in the grate and defied the winter's chill. Silently they drew their chairs toward it.

After a moment or two, Rosemary, thinking of what he had said, asked, "Why did it require courage to dismiss that man, Aubrey? It must have been maddening to have him treat you in such a manner."

He nodded. "It was my mother, primarily. She has always been a semi-invalid, and she has depended a great deal on Barron. It seemed unkind to send him away, but I simply could no longer bear it. When I heard that I had inherited your father's title, I thought that that might be the most appropriate moment to do so. If I could not work up enough courage at such a moment, then I need never think I would be able to do so."

Rosemary's load of guilt seemed to be increasing by the pound. If he had fired Barron on the strength of becoming duke, what would he think when he discovered that he was not becoming one—at least not for a while? She shuddered.

"I am sorry, Rose," he said gently, mistaking the meaning of her shudder. "I hope that he did not upset you too much."

"Well, he did make me tremendously angry, of course," she admitted frankly, "and I was delighted to see you give him such a severe setdown. He certainly deserved it."

Aubrey seemed at a temporary loss for words. Since Rosemary would learn the conditions of his inheritance sooner or later, it had seemed to him that it would be best to be candid with her before the wedding. Particularly now that she had seen Barron at his worst, she might understand more fully why he had been anxious to cut his home ties once and for all.

Bravely he took her hand. "Rose, I have not been completely honest with you," he said slowly, "and I feel that there is something that I must tell you before New Year's Day."

Her mind bounced about among various possibilities: he had another wife, he was not really Aubrey Townsend, he had murdered a man. His tone of voice made her feel that his news was weighty indeed.

She patted his hand encouragingly and thought again what a very nice young man he was. It was such a pity that she felt nothing more for him than that. Still, it was a better basis for marriage than many began with.

"According to the terms of my father's will, I have a very handsome allowance until the time that I marry. It is then that I receive my complete inheritance."

She sat and thought that over for a moment. "And so, Aubrey, you are telling me that that was the reason for your proposal to me?" she asked. "So that you could receive your full inheritance?"

His eyes dropped. "Yes, I am afraid that was the main reason."

For the first time Rosemary began to feel almost cheerful about the wedding. It appeared that she would be assisting Aubrey instead of merely victimizing him. "And what were the other reasons, Aubrey?" she asked gently.

Encouraged that she had not given any indication of an emotional response, he met her eye and continued a little shyly. "I hope that this will not offend you, Rose, but I felt that I should marry you or one of your sisters since your father had left you in such unfortunate circumstances, and I was, in effect, taking away your home."

Plunged back into guilt again, Rosemary sighed deeply and he regarded her with distress. "Did I indeed offend you, Rose?" he demanded. "I am sorry. I assure you that I never meant to do so."

"Not at all, Aubrey," she managed to reply. "I was simply impressed by your thoughtfulness, Aubrey. Not many young men would think as you did about this. It was very kind of you."

He looked at her and smiled. "Not all kind, Rosemary, it was for myself, too. You have not asked me my other reason."

"And what was that?" she asked obediently.

"That when I saw you I thought that you were the most beautiful woman I had ever seen, and then when I saw you with your family, I thought you were the kindest. So you see, my dear, that I am getting the best of the bargain."

Rosemary was now fairly crushed beneath her load of guilt. She had ensnared a young man who had been kind enough to think of offering for one of them himself. And she had done it under false pretenses, while he, thinking that she was a candid, outgoing person, had trusted her and done her the honor of telling the truth about his own situation, which he might easily have concealed until after their marriage. Only this had been lacking to make her misery complete.

"I only wish that were so, my dear," she responded gently. "I only wish that were true."

Leaving Aubrey to go upstairs and check on his mother's well-being and to undergo her strictures, Rosemary took a brief walk in the wintry gardens to calm her anger with Barron and then repaired to the bookroom again to see what he had disarranged. It was then, as she was thumbing through one of her ledgers, that the door opened with no warning.

Fully prepared to tell Mr. Barron what she thought of him, she had half risen from behind her desk before she realized that it was Barrisford in the doorway.

"I was quite sure this is where I would find you," he remarked coolly, with no hint of apology for his intrusion.

"However did Aubrey acquire such delightful manners, Lord Barrisford, when no one connected with him seems to have the faintest notion of proper conduct?" she demanded, incensed by this new invasion.

A little startled by her vehement reaction, he then remembered the conversation between him and his sister when Rosemary had entered the room without their noting it. He was only vaguely troubled by this though, feeling that her own misdeeds far outweighed their own. Carelessly he tossed the golden combs upon the desk.

"I thought that you might wish to have these again, Lady Rosemary, since they had sentimental value," he said lightly, waiting for her reaction.

Had he expected any sign of guilt, he was disappointed, however. She was expressionless as she reached out and swept them into an open drawer.

"How very gallant of you, my lord," she said. "I hope that you did not have to search too very long for them."

"No, not at all. I believe that it is simply a matter of knowing where to look," he responded, still watching her closely.

She colored slightly then, but managed to say, with a becoming air of amusement, "I think they say it is always the last place you look, my lord. The secret is in knowing what the place is so that you cut the time spent in searching."

"I was most fortunate. I went to the last place first of all," he said dryly. Then he left, closing the door gently behind him.

Rosemary sat for a long time that afternoon with the combs on the desk in front of her. What did he know? she wondered. Had he talked with the man from the *Lovely Lady*? How *had* he acquired them? Did he know about her father?

Not for the first time, Rosemary felt that her father had plunged them all into something whose outcome they could not anticipate.

Sixteen

Dinner that evening was somewhat less than a highly successful social event. Their habits at Marston Hall had been quite informal since the children had come several years ago, and, although they had made some concessions for the presence of Barrisford and Aubrey, things had gone on much as usual. The older children were once more allowed to dine with them, the younger ones had dinner earlier in the kitchen under the supervision of Mrs. O'Ryan.

Mrs. Townsend had been horrified to discover the number of children and spinsters in the household and she was even more horrified to discover that she would be sitting down to dine with the majority of them. "It is un-*civ*ilized, Aubrey!" she had protested. "Do these people know *nothing* about the *proper* way to live?"

"I think, Mother, that they consider it civilized to dine with their families," he replied calmly. "You will find the conversation intelligent and the children well behaved."

"I *can't* imagine it, Aubrey. You shall simply *have* to have a tray sent up to me tonight. I can*not* possibly sit down to dinner in such company."

"Since I am about to marry into 'this company,' Mother, I think it would be as well if you became acquainted with them. After all, when you come to visit me here, you will be sitting down to dine with them then."

Amelia gave a small shriek and fell back against her pillows. "You can't *mean* it, Aubrey! You *surely* are not clinging to that *absurd* notion of marrying this girl!"

"I most definitely am, Mother," he assured her. "And I think that if you give them a chance, you will like the Trevelyans."

Another muffled shriek was the only response, and it brought Taft hurrying into the room to give him a reproving glance.

"You know how sensitive her nerves are, my lord," she said reproachfully, waving the *sal volatile* under Amelia's nose. "I am surprised that you show so little natural feeling."

Aubrey stood up wearily. This was a little scene in which he had participated many times before. Whenever Amelia was thwarted in any manner, she had palpitations and retired to the ministrations of Taft and her doctor, leaving the thwarter to live with his guilt.

"It won't work this time, Mother," he announced as he turned to leave the room. "I will be sorry if you don't come down to dinner, but it won't change a thing. I am still going to marry Rosemary Trevelyan and her family will remain here at Marston Hall with us."

He paused at the door to deliver one final blow. "And you may tell Barron, Mother, if you see him before I do, that if he in any way intrudes himself upon the Trevelyans again, he will be asked to leave Marston Hall immediately. And I think, in view of the distress that he caused Lady Rosemary this afternoon, that it would be better if he dined in his chamber tonight."

A muffled groan echoed from behind the filmy handkerchief she had pressed to her face.

Satisfied that for once he had not backed down in the face of her palpitations, he retired to his room to dress for dinner. When he descended an hour later, he was surprised but not displeased to find his mother already dressed and downstairs. She was being ministered to by Isabella, which seemed to gratify her.

"It is so *comfortable* to be cosseted by someone who understands how *very* difficult it is for me to be away from home when I am *so* unwell," she observed in a fading voice.

There was a brief snort from Barrisford's general direction, but Amelia ignored it, choosing instead to rest gracefully on the settee of faded red velvet she had chosen as a backdrop for her gown of China blue silk, the same blue of her eyes. Isabella was occupying herself by fetching Amelia's shawl, bringing her a pillow to tuck behind her, and adjusting the screen so that the fire was not too warm for her to bear.

"You do make life almost bearable, my dear," sighed Amelia gently, in the voice of one clinging to life by a thread.

"It must be dreadful, Mrs. Townsend," murmured Isabella gently. "Suffering must surely have made you a stronger person though, so that must be some compensation."

Before Amelia could respond to this gratifying thought, her brother said in a low, but very distinct voice, to Aubrey, "If she were any stronger we would all move to India and stay there."

Isabella looked shocked, but Amelia went on grandly, quite as though she had not heard Barrisford—although she most certainly had and intended that he should pay for it—and said, "I think that *no* one truly understands pain except *those* of us who have suffered." It was fortunate that they were called in to dinner before her brother had an opportunity to comment upon this, and she allowed him to lead her in.

The cousins were quite overcome by the sophisticated Mrs. Townsend and were a little inhibited until Aubrey encouraged Merriweather to talk about the time she had spent in Ireland when she was a girl. She related one or two amusing stories from her time there with her aunt and uncle, but it was quite clear that Amelia considered Ireland a barbaric country and felt no interest in anything associated with it. Uncle Webster countered Merriweather's tales with a story of Highland revenge and Amelia made it clear that a civilized person had no truck with bloody vengeance such as he described.

"In *fact*," she concluded, "murder is to be abhorred in *any* situation. I wonder that you *tell* such stories in front of *them*, Mr. Trevelyan." And here she nodded to Robert and John, who had been drinking in every word.

"He is scarcely encouraging them, Mrs. Townsend," inserted Rosemary, weary of a guest who found fault with everyone and everything. "And as for murder, I daresay there is far more of that in London than there is in the Highlands."

Amelia looked at her crossly for a moment, then smiled sweetly. Barrisford saw her expression and knew it to be an ominous sign. "And murder *is* to be discovered in the most *un*expected places, isn't it, Lady Rosemary? Who would have *ever* expected it here at quiet Marston Hall?"

There was a moment of disbelieving silence while her words sank in, then John said, "I didn't know there had been a murder *here!*" he exclaimed. "Why hadn't we heard about it?" he demanded of Rosemary. "Why do we miss everything good?"

Amelia looked slightly ashamed of her remark. She had forgotten, in the anger of the moment, that there were children present.

"I *merely* meant that such things happen even in *quiet* places like this," she added, trying to smooth the situation over.

"There is something I must tell you all," Rosemary inserted deftly, eager to turn the conversation. "Mrs. Tipton came to call this afternoon, and she and her husband wish to have a party tomorrow night in honor of our approaching marriage. Aubrey and I thought that it was delightful of them to do this for us, and we accepted."

"Are we all invited?" asked John skeptically.

"Yes, of course, you are," responded Rosemary. "This is a family affair. Of course, you will have to dress for the occasion and behave wonderfully well."

The boys both groaned, but it was clear that they were gratified to be included.

It was also clear, however, that Amelia was anything but gratified. She said nothing, but words were not necessary; her strained expression said everything. When the tablecloth was removed and the ladies withdrew to the drawing room, she announced abruptly that she had the headache and retired to her room. Isabella offered to bring her some hot milk or another posset, but Amelia refused her rather sharply.

When she had left, Rosemary observed, "Well, it will be a much more pleasant evening now."

"Rose!" Isabella reproved her. "You know that Mrs. Townsend is not feeling well. Much can be forgiven those who are ill."

"But you are never cross, Bella; even when you were much sicker than she appears to be," pointed out Candace practically.

"Well, that is because Bella is never cross, Candace. You know that," retorted Anne. "When have you ever heard her say an angry word?"

"I have noticed that, too," said Aubrey, the first of the gentlemen to enter the room. "It is quite a remarkable thing to be so even-tempered, Bella."

Isabella blushed and turned away, but Rosemary observed fondly, "She has always been that way. Even when she was a tiny child, she was the peacemaker, the one who wanted everyone to like everyone else. And she is still trying, never recognizing what a hopeless task it is."

"It isn't hopeless, Rose!" she exclaimed. "You know that. Many times people do kind things for one another."

"You see what I mean?" said Rosemary with a smile, turning to Aubrey. But he was studying Isabella's face and did not look up. "Yes, I think I do," he said, finally pulling his eyes from hers.

Rosemary was mesmerized by what she saw there. Aubrey was falling in love with Bella. And, if she knew anything about Bella, it was very likely that she returned his affection. Then she remembered their situation and groaned inwardly. What a coil! she thought to herself. And here am I, between them.

As she looked up again, she saw Barrisford's eyes fixed on her face. Then he glanced at Aubrey and Bella and smiled. Despicable man! she thought to herself. He still thinks he is going to disrupt the wedding and whisk Aubrey away.

She thought of the gold combs and wondered why he had returned them to her—and how he had gotten them. Quite deliberately she had worn them tonight, hoping for some sort of reaction from him. She knew that he had been aware of them, for his eyes had strayed to them, but he had given no indication of what he thought.

She was finding it more and more difficult to play the role that had been selected for her. Aubrey deserved the truth and the opportunity to choose his bride honestly. She was winning him with deceit, a quality alien to her nature. And now to see that he and Bella were falling in love—well, it was all past praying for now. She wished that she could talk to her father for a moment to at least try to convince him to think of another way out of their predicament.

She and Matilda were the only ones left in the drawing room when Mrs. O'Ryan came in later that night.

"Lady Rosemary, there's a man at the servants' entrance asking to speak with you. I told him that it was too late, he should come back tomorrow, but he insisted that you would see him now." Mrs. O'Ryan's hands were twisting her apron, a sure sign of an agitated mind.

"Did he give his name?" Rosemary asked, immediately filled with a feeling of foreboding.

Mrs. O'Ryan shook her head. "He insisted that you wouldn't need a name and that you'd see him."

"Is he in the kitchen?" Rosemary asked, starting toward the door.

"No, my lady. I wouldn't let the likes of him stay in the house without me there to watch him. I made him stay outside and I locked the door."

"I'm sure that was very wise of you, Mrs. O'Ryan. Thank you." Rosemary thought quickly, and knew that she had no desire to face the sailor alone and late at night—particularly when she had nothing else to give him. Then her mind gave a sudden lurch—her sapphires—she had almost forgotten them.

She frowned, however, for she knew that

there was no guarantee that this would satisfy him. Perhaps for the moment, until his next time back in port when he had spent it all. Then he would be back again.

"Mrs. O'Ryan, I want you to go to the back door and call to him. Don't unlock the door, just call out and tell him that I have no desire to speak to him this late at night."

Mrs. O'Ryan nodded with some semblance of satisfaction. "I told him it was too late to be bothering people. But I don't think, Lady Rosemary, that you should see him at all. He'd look just as dreadful in the sunlight—or very likely worse."

Rosemary was very inclined to agree with her housekeeper, and she was very uncomfortable at the thought that such a man was wandering about outside the house. It was too cold, however, so he would probably take himself back to the inn very soon. Tomorrow she would decide what to do about him.

When Rosemary went in to say good night to Mrs. O'Ryan a little later, the housekeeper pursed her lips together and said, "I've never heard such a stream of curses in my life, my lady, as I did when I gave him your message."

"I'm terribly sorry you were bothered by him, Mrs. O'Ryan," said Rosemary remorsefully.

"Not a bit of it," the housekeeper said briskly. "I'd far rather that I was doing the talking to him than a young lady like yourself.

You have no business being next or nigh to someone like that."

Rosemary found herself in total agreement with Mrs. O'Ryan, thanked her again, and then walked slowly up to bed. Her father's simple solution to their problem had spawned more difficulties than she could handle and she longed to place her burden on someone else's shoulders. Unfortunately, there was no one else save Julian, and this was not really his problem at all—just more Trevelyan troubles to be laid on his plate. It would be a miracle if he ever decided that he wanted to offer for Anne since it would mean marrying into them and inheriting all of the problems. No, he would be very wise to stay completely away from them.

The hours slipped by that night, but sleep would not come to her. Finally, desperate for some relief, she decided that a little fresh air might help her. Slipping on an old woolen cloak over her nightdress, she made her way quietly down to the side door, unlocked and unbolted it, and stepped out onto the terrace that overlooked the lake.

The air was icy, but the beauty of the night caught at her throat. Shadows dappled the moonlit snow, and everything was perfectly still. She sighed. Here, at least, everything was peaceful.

Then the door opened again and Lord Barrisford stepped out onto the terrace with her.

Rosemary wrapped her cloak more tightly about her and stared at him defiantly.

"Are you keeping track of my every move? Have you come to see if I am on my way to the lake, my lord?" She held up her hands. "You see, they are empty. I am carrying no skates."

He shook his head. "No, I am aware that you are staying here tonight, Lady Rosemary." Then he added, "I saw your earlier guest leave the grounds after I went up to my chamber. Not a very savory-looking character to have about the place."

Rosemary shook her head in agreement but said nothing more about the sailor. Barrisford was an unaccountable man; if he knew all about the sailor, he was playing a waiting game and she would give him no other information. He would doubtless act whenever he thought right and she would not worry about it until she knew exactly what she must worry about.

Then, after they had stood there quietly for a few minutes admiring the night, Rose asked abruptly, "Do you still think I am a murderess, my lord? I note that your sister is probably convinced of it."

She waited for him to respond, but the moments ticked by slowly and he still did not answer. Rosemary determined that she would not break the silence for him. If anything more were said, it would have to come from him.

233

Finally, he said slowly, "I wonder still how you truly came by that ring—and I wonder about how secure Aubrey will be after you bear him an heir."

She stared at him in astonishment as the meaning of his words sank in. When she raised her hand to slap him, he caught her wrist and pulled her to him, speaking softly into her ear.

"Did you know, my dear, that I, too, am a wealthy man—wealthier even than Aubrey? I could not make you a duchess, of course, but I think that that does not matter to you as much as the money does."

Despising himself for his weakness, he took her into his arms and kissed her, but she pulled away from him and ran back into the house. Angry at himself, angry at her, he called after her: "If you had been the woman you seemed to be, I could have truly loved you!"

Left alone in the cold, Barrisford pulled the ring out of his pocket and examined it gently. As he looked at it, it began to dawn upon him that he could force her to marry him now. A little blackmail would do it. If she married him, Aubrey would be safe and Amelia finally satisfied and Rosemary would have the wealth she apparently desired. And—he admitted to himself finally—it would give him Rosemary. By the time he retired to bed that night, he had determined that he would do exactly

that—force her to marry him. It was for the
good of everyone involved. And, feeling quite
saintly, he prepared for bed.

Seventeen

Rosemary was so incensed by Barrisford's questions that she could scarcely sleep the rest of the night. It was unbelievable that he should think her capable not only of murdering her own father, but now Aubrey as well! But not, of course, until there was a male heir—or perhaps two—so that Marston Hall and the dukedom stayed within her control.

"A pretty sort of woman he must think me!" she said to her glass, jerking her brush through her hair the next morning. And yet, thinking all of those things about her, he still wanted to marry her—or so he said. It was probably a ruse to lure her away from Aubrey so that Barrisford could then abandon her with a smile and ask how she ever could have dreamed he had been serious.

Now and then, however, his final words echoed through her mind. If she had been the kind of woman he had at first thought, he could have loved her. Well, it was unfortunate that she was no longer the kind of person she once had been—prior to her father's splendid idea for solving their problems.

By the time she went down to breakfast, she had determined that she would be as charming and gracious to Aubrey as she possibly could be. She would allow him to take the lead in all things—if she could remember to. She would defer to his opinion prettily. In short, she would make Aubrey a happy man in the hopes that Barrisford would grind his teeth to a powder while he watched. The thought of that sent her into the dining room with a glowing smile.

"Good morning, everyone," she chirped as she entered. "Everyone" at that moment consisted of Aubrey, Uncle Webster, Barrisford, Merriweather, and Candace. The younger children had already eaten and their morning merriment could be heard echoing faintly from the precincts of the kitchen.

To the astonishment of those gathered, she bent down and kissed Aubrey on the cheek. Since she was not prone to public displays of affection, even Aubrey looked up in surprise, but it was plain that he was gratified.

"Good morning, Rose," he said, smiling at her and standing to pull out her chair for her. "How lovely you look this morning."

"How charming of you to say so, Aubrey dear." Her voice was virtually a coo. "What would you like to do today?"

He looked at her a little blankly. The normal morning procedure had been for Rosemary to inform him of her schedule for the day, and he could decide which things he would do with her. There had, of course, been lessons about the estate interspersed throughout the other activities, and it had always been perfectly clear that Rosemary was the one in charge.

"Well, I hadn't thought about it, Rose—that is, I hadn't yet decided," he added hurriedly. "It may be that your ring will arrive today. I ordered it from London and they are to send a special messenger here with it."

Rosemary smiled warmly. "How lovely of you, Aubrey! If it came today, then I could wear it to the Tiptons' party tonight."

Barrisford had been watching this display of affection very dourly. "I had not thought of the matter of a ring, Aubrey," he said slowly, "or I could have told you that you could wait on that matter. I have a very handsome ring with me that you might have used."

Aubrey turned to him, his eyebrows raised. "Whyever are you carrying about a ring with you, Uncle?

Rosemary interceded hurriedly with a sharp little laugh. "I imagine that Lord Barrisford must always be prepared with a ring just in case the fancy strikes him to propose to someone."

The thought of Barrisford wandering about

the country with an engagement ring handily tucked away in his pocket seemed to offer his nephew a great deal of pleasure. When his laughter subsided and he had wiped his eyes on his napkin, he turned to Rosemary to explain.

"You must understand, Rose, that my uncle is not, apparently, one of the marrying kind. The ladies try in vain to lead him to the altar, but he will have none of it. It would be much more likely that the ladies would come prepared with a ring."

Rosemary smiled faintly, but her attention was occupied by Barrisford, whose eyes had met hers as his hand strayed to his waistcoat pocket. Surely he would not bring out her father's ring here. She finally drew a breath when he returned his hand to the business of breakfast and smiled knowingly at her. Doubtless they would be playing this cat and mouse game all the way to New Year's Day.

Aubrey, in the meantime, had gone back to her original question and had decided that they would go for a brief walk in the morning so that Lady Isabella could have a bit of exercise, and then they could go to the village for Mrs. O'Ryan, who was busily preparing for the wedding festivities on New Year's Day.

"And when we come back, my dear," he explained somewhat apologetically, "I must spend some time with the children. I had promised them that I would skate with them for a while. Perhaps you would like to join us."

Rosemary smiled. "We shall see, Aubrey. Do remember that since the weather has warmed a bit and the sun has been out, the children should not skate in the middle. Check the ice carefully, but the part closest to the perimeter should be safe."

"Yes, of course, I will make them be cautious. Will you not be coming with us then?" he asked.

"Since there is the party tonight, I may rest this afternoon." What she must do, she knew, was to speak to her father. Things seemed to have gotten completely out of hand, and she needed to speak to someone aside from Julian about the problems that were arising thick and fast.

There was the matter of the sailor, too. If Mrs. O'Ryan answered the door when he came, she could be trusted to put him safely away where she could talk to him in privacy, although what she was to say to him, she had no idea. That was another question for her father. But if one of the others answered the door, they would wish to know who this man was and what he wanted—and she would be hard-pressed to answer. Well, she thought, one step at a time. I will do what I can.

The morning passed peacefully enough. They went for their walk, with Aubrey shepherding Isabella carefully down the drive and the children rolling down the slopes and throwing snowballs until they looked like snowballs themselves. To her surprise, Barrisford accompanied them on the stroll, and as Isabella stopped to point out the tree from which Will had fallen to Aubrey, he came to stand by Rosemary.

"They make a lovely couple, do they not, Lady Rosemary?" he said in a disinterested voice, looking at Aubrey and Bella. She had just been thinking a very similar thing herself. Bella, quiet and gentle, looked to Aubrey to guide her, and Aubrey, unaccustomed to being depended upon, responded warmly. Still, she did not appreciate his comment and she turned to him with raised eyebrows.

"Whatever do you mean, Lord Barrisford?" she asked carelessly, and strolled on as though the whole matter had nothing to do with her. She would have dearly loved to have taken one of the children's snowballs and used it upon the man. He had such an infuriatingly smug expression!

"I daresay Lady Isabella will miss Aubrey when he has gone," Barrisford added, joining her again.

"Why, where is Aubrey going that Bella should miss him?"

"I was thinking of the future, Lady Rosemary—after you have your heir."

Rosemary knew that she could not make a scene by attempting to slap him, so she smiled gently and said, "I wonder that you could so underestimate my cautiousness, Lord Barrisford. I assure you that nothing would happen until there were at least *two* male heirs. So you see, Bella will not be deprived for some time to come."

"How very farsighted of you, ma'am," he replied, looking down at her in amusement. "You are right; I did underestimate your caution. You may depend upon it that I shall not do so again."

After their walk Rosemary excused herself to go up to her chamber to rest. There was no comment from the rest of the group other than Candace, who looked up curiously and asked, "Are you feeling quite all right, Rose? You never rest in the afternoon."

She noticed with annoyance that Barrisford looked up sharply at this remark, but she replied smoothly, "I have the headache, Candace, but it will soon go away if I drink one of Merriweather's tisanes and rest for a while."

Delighted to be of service, Merriweather bustled off to the kitchen, and Rosemary went quietly to her room, hoping that she had laid his suspicions to rest. All that she needed this afternoon was for Barrisford to follow her.

After Merriweather had brought her a cup of camomile tea, strengthened with a few special ingredients of her own, Rosemary allowed her to close the draperies and spread a cover over her. Merriweather began to tiptoe lightly from the room, then remembering something, tiptoed back.

"Rose," she whispered, as though she expected Rosemary to be asleep already.

"Yes, Merriweather?" she replied, not opening her eyes.

"I took Mrs. Townsend one of my special tisanes this morning, too. Do you think that it was presumptuous of me to do so?"

"Not at all, Merriweather. It was very kind of you. I'm sure that Mrs. Townsend appreciated it."

"Well, I wasn't certain. I thought that I heard her say, 'What *is* that?' to her maid as I was closing the door. Do you think that I should go and check on her? She hasn't been down all day."

Rosemary smiled to herself. "Yes, indeed, Merriweather. I think that you should show her every attention. She is, after all, in very poor health and you could be very helpful to her."

She enjoyed picturing Mrs. Townsend's expression when she received another cup of Merriweather's potent brew and Merriweather's full attention. There was no one that Merriweather loved more than an invalid.

Merriweather brightened immediately at Rosemary's words. "Well, I will certainly do so. And I will tell her that it was your suggestion so that she knows that you were the one thinking of her comfort."

"Yes, you do that, Merriweather."

And Merriweather went bustling happily out, ready to render horrible Mrs. Townsend's sickbed.

"I daresay she shall be up and about in no time," Rosemary murmured to herself.

After she was quite certain that she would not be bothered again, Rosemary closed the curtains around her bed so that no one just peeking into the room would realize that she had left. Then she changed into woolen stockings and gown and an old-fashioned, heavy cape. It was cold out today, and she did not want a chill. Catching up her ice skates, which she had handily secured in her room, she set off for the lake.

Slipping out the side door next to her office, she hurried to place herself behind a tall hedge and walked the long way around to the lake, taking a path that wound around for a while, then came close to the lake after a walk through the woods. She checked over her shoulder constantly, but she saw no sign that she was being followed. Instead of going out onto the ice where they normally skated, she went farther up into the woods and slipped out onto the ice at a point that was out of sight of the Hall. Keeping well to the side where she knew the ice was firm, she made her way quickly along the shore.

The trip was a brisk one, and she was relieved to stop and rest when she came to Melrose Manor. She sat down on a bench close to the ice which was sheltered from the wind by a stand of evergreens, and watched for any sign of Barrisford's following her. When she was quite certain she was alone, she began again, this time at a spanking pace. Another ten minutes brought her within sight of a cottage tucked away in the fold between two small hills.

She could see that her father was there—as he was supposed to be—because smoke curled cheerfully from the chimney. Julian had settled him here to keep him out of sight and out of trouble until the marriage was final. There was to be little contact between Rosemary and her father because of the danger of being discovered, and even Julian went to the cottage rarely so that he would not attract attention to the place. He did check occasionally, however, to bring provisions and so that he could tell Rosemary that all was well—or as well as it could be under the circumstances.

As she approached the cottage, she could see that things were not just as she had pictured them. It was obvious that other people had been there, for there were carriage tracks and horses' hooves in the snow, and she could hear the snorting and pawing of a horse from within a large shed to one side of the cottage. Julian might have ridden over, but he would have had only one horse, and he would never have driven over in a carriage.

Rosemary approached the door cautiously and knocked. Her father threw open the door and beamed at her.

"Rosemary! My darling daughter!" he exclaimed, stretching out his arms and enfolding her. He had never called her such a thing before, she reflected. The fact that she was marrying Aubrey must account for the new rush of affection on her father's part. As she peered over his shoulder, her eyes widened, for there was a card table drawn up beside a cozy fire and there sat three men, all strangers to her.

"Father!" she whispered sharply. "Who *are* those men?"

He looked surprised for a moment, then replied, "Oh, forgive me, my dear. I had forgotten that you would not know them. This gentleman," he said, indicating a tall, rather sallow man wearing a long black wig, "is Lord Findlay. The wicked-looking fellow beside him is Henry Sayers, and the one in the corner is Dudley Raxton. Gentlemen, this is my eldest daughter, Lady Rosemary."

The gentlemen stood and bowed, although Raxton had to struggle to extricate himself from his corner. "I am delighted to meet you, my dear," he managed to say after gaining his feet.

"At your service, my lady," murmured Lord Findlay, taking her hand and bowing over it.

"I would have known you as your father's child without the introduction," said Henry

Sayers, his eyes bright with mischief. "You have exactly the look of him, although, of course, you have no gray hairs scattered among your dark ones."

Having acknowledged their greetings, Rosemary managed to take her father's arm and guide him to one side.

"Father," she whispered urgently. "You said that you were to keep your plan a secret. Why have you told all of these men?"

Her father looked a little shamefaced. "And I intended to, my dear, but I am simply not accustomed to being walled up in a rural prison like this, and Baxter is no hand at cards."

"You have Baxter here, too?" she demanded.

Trevelyan looked a little shocked. "Well, naturally I brought my valet, Rosemary. I am not giving up living—I am merely in seclusion for a while. And Baxter already knew all about it because he helped me to make my arrangements."

Baxter appeared in the doorway just then, carrying a tray with refreshments for the gentlemen.

"And when I found that I was simply not going to be able to stay here without any company, it occurred to me that my very good friends might consent to come to my rescue. I sent Baxter to them and they arrived on Christmas Eve. I thought it very noble of them to forgo the pleasures of the town and come to minister to me."

Rosemary looked at the group at the table. None of them appeared to be the sort of personality associated with ministering angels.

"Will they keep your secret, Father?" she demanded. "After all that we have been through, will they?"

"Yes, yes, of course they will," he responded, offended by her doubt. "They know that everything rides upon your marriage."

Hearing his final words, Henry Sayers called out, "And we wish to salute you, Lady Rosemary, upon your coming nuptials. We wish you every happiness." And so saying, he stood and lifted his glass to her. The others followed suit and drank to her happiness.

"In fact, my dear, so pleased are we for you—and for your father, of course—that we plan to attend the wedding ourselves, providing that it will not inconvenience you to allow us to be your guests."

Actually, there was scarcely anything that appealed to her less, but she could not see how to refuse them, so she smilingly indicated that she would be delighted to have them honor her wedding with their presence.

Finally, determined to have a word alone with her father, she took him by the arm and virtually dragged him into the kitchen.

"Father, I must talk to you privately about

all of this! I cannot feel that this is the correct thing to do," she began.

"But of course it is the correct thing to do," he said, astonished that she could doubt it. "How else could we keep Marston Hall?"

"But, Father, Aubrey and Bella are in love!"

"Bella?" he said blankly.

"Your daughter Isabella," she reminded him briskly. "She is in love with Aubrey Townsend and it appears to me that he loves her also."

Trevelyan looked thoughtful for a moment. "Do you think they would marry?" he inquired. "If they had the chance, that is?"

"I think it is very possible, Father, but I cannot be certain."

He shook his head regretfully. "That is too bad then. We must have a wedding and it must be very soon. Since you are engaged, you must be the one."

Then, seeing her expression, he added helpfully, "They will get over it, you know, my dear. People always do."

"Another problem is Lord Barrisford, Father."

"I do not find that difficult to believe. Being a problem is what he does best."

"I think that he will do everything within his power to stop my wedding, and—" Here she hesitated a moment, then continued. "He says, Father, that he would like to marry me and that he is a wealthier man than Aubrey."

"And so he is," replied her father in

astonishment. "But—Barrisford! Are you quite sure you heard him correctly, my dear? He *was* asking you to *marry* him?"

"Oh, yes, he was very clear—although he clearly considers me a murderess, too."

"A murderess?" her father exclaimed. "Why, what have you been doing, Rosemary?"

She was growing impatient. "I have been doing what you told me to, Father. But Barrisford suspects me of murdering you, perhaps with Julian's help, and he thinks that I might murder Aubrey after I had given birth to a male heir."

"Is the man mad?" gasped Trevelyan. "To think that a daughter of mine—a Trevelyan—could be guilty of such an atrocity!"

Rosemary couldn't decide whether to laugh or to cry, but instead she said quietly, "I believe that it is *because* I am a Trevelyan that he thinks such a thing is possible."

"Well, then, he surely cannot seriously be offering marriage, my dear. No man would marry a female whom he suspected of murder. He would never know whether or not he would wake up the next morning. So you still must marry Townsend, my child."

"And did Julian tell you that Barrisford now has your ring?" she asked.

"He is a bothersome fellow!" snapped Trevelyan. "He must have nothing better to do than to sniff about in other people's business. But don't worry about it. Once I return, he will give it back to me, and that will be an end to all of it."

Rosemary wished that she felt that certain of the outcome, but she made one last attempt to fix her father's wandering attention. "And there is a sailor from the *Lucky Lady*, Father, who says that he knows all about the whole thing, and he is blackmailing us."

She could see that she had succeeded in recapturing his attention. "Who is 'us,' Rosemary?"

"Julian and I," she responded. "Julian gave him some money and I gave him Mother's antique gold combs—although Barrisford got them back somehow. But then the sailor came around late last night and wanted more, but I sent him away because it was too late for me to come down. What am I to do when he comes again today, Father? A payment won't keep him away."

"Just so, my dear. That kind will keep turning up, like a bad penny. Baxter will take care of him tonight, Rosemary. He is a very capable fellow, Baxter, and we may trust him with anything."

"Very well, Father," she responded, giving him a dutiful peck on the cheek and preparing to return to the ice to skate home. She must be back in plenty of time to allow her color to fade before dressing for dinner, or everyone would know that she had been outside.

When Jack Trevelyan returned to his guests,

they complimented him on his handsome daughter. "Young Townsend is making an excellent bargain," said Sayers. "I hope that he is worthy of her."

"Well, we soon shall know, gentlemen," said Raxton heartily. "After all, when we arrive tomorrow as guests for the wedding, we shall have ample time to form our own opinions of the young man."

"*And* of his card playing," added Lord Findlay in a tone fraught with meaning.

"Just so," agreed Raxton. "After such a long wait, I'm sure that playing cards with Aubrey Townsend will be well worth our time."

Eighteen

In the eyes of almost everyone who attended, the Tiptons' impromptu social to celebrate the approaching wedding was a great success. It was felt that Arthur Tipton toasted the betrothed pair with extraordinary wit and charm, and Uncle Webster followed that with a tribute to Lady Rosemary and her winning ways, a tribute that was widely applauded since she was a general favorite.

There was little more that could be asked of a betrothal party. The engaged couple were handsome and well liked, the young man wealthy and generous, the food and wine were excellent, the company congenial. The Tiptons had hired a small orchestra and cleared their two drawing rooms of furniture so that there would be enough room to dance; there were card tables set up in the library and refreshments loaded the dining room table and sideboard.

Even Amelia had ventured forth, accompanied by Barron, and she held court in a corner where Mrs. Tipton, hearing of her weakened state, had arranged the most comfortable chair and foot stool for the invalid. Well provided with a plate of delicacies and a glass of champagne, Amelia indicated to Isabella and Barron that she thought she would be able to remain for the evening if she exercised great strength of will.

"I would do anything for my dear son," she told Isabella soulfully, and Isabella of course agreed. Who would not do anything that they could for Aubrey?

Together they watched the dancers, and it was not long before Isabella was led out on the arm of a handsome young man who had come to visit Arthur. Rosemary was pleased to take note of that, but she also noticed with displeasure that Barrisford had taken the arm of a lovely young matron. Turning to Aubrey, she smiled brightly and did her best to make glittering conversation whenever it was possible to do so.

Aubrey, a little overwhelmed by the full force of her charm, forgot Isabella for the moment and concentrated his attention on Rosemary, who was, after all, about to become his bride. He was pleased that his mother had come and that she had apparently given up the thought of stopping their marriage. It would be, he thought, a very satisfactory marriage. Rosemary was lovely and charming and, if she was a little too strong-willed at times, that was something that would change with time. He felt certain that he could take charge of things now. His thoughts lingered with Isabella for a moment, but he reminded himself that a gentleman could not cry off from one marriage, now very much publicized, and then marry the sister of the young woman he had forsaken. At least he would be able to see Isabella.

Seeing Isabella just at the moment, however, wasn't making him particularly happy. Her partner was a broad-shouldered young man who laughed too often and seemed to admire Isabella a little too much. She is probably growing tired, he thought, and wished he had the right to tell her she must sit down and rest now beside his mother.

With a start, he realized that Rosemary was speaking to him, and he reminded himself that he was virtually a bridegroom and that he had a part to play. He looked down into her shining eyes and smiled, looking far more cheerful than he felt.

"Are you happy, Rose?" he asked tenderly.

"Oh, yes, Aubrey. Indeed I am," she replied, hoping that sincerity rang in every tone. When she saw Barrisford with his plump young matron, she desired nothing so much as to tread sharply upon his foot. She looked down at her small, flat-soled slipper. Unfortunately, that would not inflict the pain that she would wish.

Perhaps if there were small spikes on the sole. . . . And on that happy thought she smiled soulfully at Aubrey, causing him to think again that she was the best-tempered young woman he had ever met.

Mrs. Tipton had arranged for them to have a waltz, too, that scandalous dance that had finally made its way to the more rural parts of the land. Doubtless Barrisford would stand up for that with his matron, all blond curls and plump curves. She was shocked, therefore, when, with Isabella on his arm, he neatly rearranged the partners so that Aubrey was leading Isabella onto the floor while she was on Barrisford's arm.

"How charming you look tonight, Lady Rosemary," he said blandly. "Claret is a color that you wear to perfection."

"Thank you, Lord Barrisford," she responded primly. "It is the favored color of murderesses for obvious reasons; there is so little likelihood of telltale stains."

"I suppose that you are going to hold that against me forever," he sighed.

"At least that long," she assured him. Then, thinking over his words, she added, "Do you mean that you no longer believe that to be true?"

"Not at all, Lady Rosemary. I was merely making an observation," he responded. "Nothing has happened to cause me to alter my opinion."

Thinking fondly of the spikes, Rosemary looked up into his cool gray eyes. He was absolutely unruffled and, to all appearances, incapable of being ruffled. She wondered for a moment what it would take to shake him from his cool composure and his certainty that he must be correct about everything.

"Have you never been wrong, Lord Barrisford?" she inquired tartly.

He remembered Maria and his eyes clouded for a moment, but he replied smoothly, "So seldom that it is not worth remarking upon."

"How very nice for you and how inconvenient for anyone closely connected with you," she observed.

"I have no one closely connected with me," he returned. "I prefer it that way."

"Do you indeed?" she asked, genuinely surprised. "I would have thought that you would enjoy having an admiring throng about you that you could trample into the earth at will."

"Hardly," he replied, amused. "I can think of nothing that appeals to me less. If that is what you think, you have misread my character entirely. I prefer to be unfettered."

She did not reply, but satisfied herself with studying his face. She had not thought of him in such a light. From the admiration that Aubrey felt for him, she had thought that he enjoyed ordering about the impressionable young, delivering strictures on behavior. Apparently not.

"You make me feel, Lady Rosemary, as though I have been weighed in the balance and found wanting," he said, finally breaking the silence as she openly studied him.

"I am trying to decide, Lord Barrisford," she said seriously. "But I don't think I can decide as yet."

"Then I shall hope," he said lightly.

At that moment, she looked up and saw Aubrey and Isabella together, Bella's face glowing as she looked up at her partner, and with a rush her whole problem came flooding back. She might be distracted for a few moments by a practiced flirt such as Barrisford, but Aubrey was her fiancé, and the wedding must take place. She remembered angrily that Barrisford had been responsible for this change of partners, and had left the two youngsters to the intimacy of this new dance, thus exposing them to the possibility of more heartbreak. They must be kept apart as much as possible so that Bella could be spared.

When the dance was over, Rosemary returned immediately to Aubrey and monopolized his attention for the rest of the evening. Surely Bella would get over this soon, she told herself—if only another eligible young man would come along, she would forget Aubrey. And if Rosemary married Aubrey, she would be in a position to see to it that Bella had such opportunities.

Barrisford watched with irritation as Rosemary drew Aubrey to her and kept him there. It was quite unnecessary, he thought, to make such a spectacle of being engaged. At the close of the evening, when the Tiptons ceremonially brought in a new kissing bough specially designed for the occasion, there was a round of applause, and it was hung above the heads of the happy couple. After a good many comments and hints, Aubrey took Rosemary in his arms and kissed her warmly. Barrisford turned away—and as he did so, he saw Bella slip from the room, wiping her eyes.

The next morning offered no respite from the loverlike behavior of Aubrey and Rosemary. She clung to him in what Barrisford could only describe to himself as a cloying manner, and he left the breakfast table early rather than be exposed to it. There seemed to be no respite from it, however, for wherever he turned that day, they were there.

Finally, in desperation, he sought his sister's room, for he knew that Rosemary would not pursue him there—or at least he did not think that she would.

"Well, Robert," commented Amelia, "it seems to *me* that if you *really* plan to put a stop to this wedding, you are going about it in an *unconscionably* roundabout manner. By the time you *do* something about it, they will have *six* children."

"You exaggerate, Amelia," he returned calmly, plucking a teacake from the tray.

"And for the *Banbury* story you told me about *your* planning to marry the chit, I can't think of *anything* more ridiculous in my life. What *are* you going to do, Robert?"

"You will see, Amelia."

"Now *that* is the most infuriating thing you have said to me *yet*. Why won't you tell me *what* you are going to do?"

Since he had no inclination to tell her that he had no idea exactly how he was going to take care of the problem, he maintained his enigmatic silence.

He was saved from more questions by the sound of a carriage on the drive, and he strolled to the window to look out. What he saw brought an oath to his lips and Amelia looked up, startled.

"What *is* it, Robert? What do you see?"

"Three of Jack Trevelyan's cronies—Findlay, Raxton, and Sayers—with their luggage."

Her hand flew to her lips. "Not staying *here*, Robert! *Surely* not staying here where Aubrey is. *Not* after the trouble we've taken to keep him *away* from their kind."

"From the look of it, they are very much here. Undoubtedly for the wedding, although how they devil they came to hear of it, I don't know!"

"You *must* go downstairs immediately, Robert. *I* will get dressed and come down myself as *soon* as it is possible. We *must* not leave them alone with Aubrey for a *moment*."

"They won't be," he assured her. "I will see to that."

And he was as good as his word. No matter what the three of them did for the next few hours, Aubrey was never left unattended. Finally, in the late afternoon, Aubrey adjourned to the lake to ice-skate with the children.

"Would you care to join us, gentlemen?" he smilingly inquired of the three.

Raxton repressed a visible shudder that shook his plump frame. "Definitely not, Barrisford! Definitely not!" he assured them.

Certain that, for the moment at least, he had them stymied, Barrisford joined the group at the lake. As he fastened his skates, he saw Rosemary clinging to Aubrey's arm and gazing soulfully up at him. A quick glance thrown in his direction made him quite sure that this was, at least in part, a performance for him. Determined to ignore them, he tried to concentrate on his plan of action for blocking the marriage.

As he skated, hands caught thoughtfully behind him, he glided along the perimeter of firm ice, carefully avoiding the center where the ice had grown thin and begun to crack. Finally, he began to grow a little calmer. The children began to gather themselves together and return to the house, and Barron came down to summon Aubrey to his mother's side. Relieved for the moment of his duty as watchdog, he dipped into a tiny cove and sat down on a rock close to the ice to think his problem through.

Thus it was that when Rosemary slipped back down to the lake alone, she was unaware of his presence until she skated directly by him. He had seen her coming and had determined that he would seize his opportunity now. As she skated by him, he emerged quickly from the lengthening shadows.

Startled, she smothered a shriek and looked at him with large, dark eyes. "Why are you springing out of the shadows, my lord?" she demanded tartly, annoyed by the fright he had given her. "Have you nothing to do other than play nursery games?"

"It is getting late for you to be out, Lady Rosemary—particularly out alone. Or were you meeting someone?" he inquired abruptly, remembering some of her other adventures on the lake when she appeared to be alone.

"Of course not," she said sharply. But he had seen her glance inadvertently flicker across the lake. "However, Lord Barrisford, I do wish to be alone."

She turned to skate away, but he caught her arm. "Rosemary, you *are* going to marry me!" he announced, glaring down at her.

"You have such a charming manner, my lord," she said sweetly. "It does not amaze me at all that you are still a bachelor. I would like to remind you that I am about to marry your nephew."

"No, you are not," he insisted. "You have no choice."

"I beg your pardon?" she snapped. "Of course I have a choice! I cannot imagine who has let you behave in such a highhanded manner and get away with it. What would make you say such a muttonheaded thing?"

Not being accustomed to thinking of himself as a muttonhead, Barrisford's reaction was scarcely gracious. Strengthening his grip on her arm, he said in a low voice, "If you *don't* marry me, Rosemary, I will make a scandal of the matter of the ring—and you know that I could do it."

"As I am sure you know, Lord Barrisford, my family has scarcely been a stranger to scandal. From first to last, we have done outrageous things. Why should we behave in another manner now?" She was pale, but very composed, and her composure enraged him all the more.

"I would remind you, my fine lady, that you would lose Aubrey if this story became known. And then what would become of your family?"

She was silent, for she knew that he was correct. Taking advantage of the moment, he pressed harder. "You cannot be allowed to marry Aubrey, but *I* am willing to marry you— and that would save your family, you know."

She looked at him in disbelief. "And why would you marry me, my lord? After all, you believe me to be a murderess, so why would you consider marrying me?"

"I think you know the answer to that, Rosemary. Of course, there is one stipulation that I would make when we marry."

"What?" she demanded. "That I promise not to put arsenic in your tea?"

Ignoring her sarcasm, he continued, "You must give up your lover. There can be no more meetings with Julian Melrose."

Looking at him in disbelief, she jerked her arm away and began to skate rapidly away. Surprised by her sudden movement, it took him a moment to get into motion—and to realize that she was heading for the middle of the lake and the thin ice. He called out to her, but she appeared not to hear and plunged ahead.

He knew that he could never catch her, but he began skating furiously in that direction, calling her name. A sudden, sickening cracking of the ice rang out like a pistol shot, and Rosemary disappeared into the black pool of water suddenly exposed by the parting of the ice.

Calling wildly for help, but knowing that everyone was safely within the house, he skated as close as he dared, and then stretched out full length on the ice, trying to reach her. Her head had bobbed back up, and she was attempting to brace herself on the edge of the ice.

"Put out your arm, Rosemary!" he shouted. "Reach for me!"

She released her grip with one hand and tried to reach him, but it was clear that it was not going to do.

"Barrisford!" When he looked up, he saw a dark figure skating rapidly toward him across the ice, carrying a long branch. "Use this!" the figure called to him, finally getting close enough to slide the branch to him.

Barrisford stared at the newcomer without speaking as he picked up the branch. It was Jack Trevelyan, the fifth Duke of Stedham.

Nineteen

Barrisford had no opportunity to reflect on this startling resurrection at the time. Between them, he and Stedham finally managed to pull Rosemary from the icy water, but it was a long and arduous process. Rosemary was small and slender, but she was wearing a woolen cloak whose weight had increased many times over once it was waterlogged.

By the time they freed her, she was barely conscious and Barrisford feared that they might have taken too long. He tore the sodden cloak from her and wrapped her in his own jacket, while her father used his to cover her wet hair and shoulders. Together they raced across the ice, not even pausing at the edge to remove their skates. Finally, the clumsiness of their movements forced them to stop, Stedham kneeling to unstrap Barrisford's skates so that he could continue, for he refused to give Rosemary to her father.

John and Robert had seen them coming, so

the household was alerted immediately and the better portion of its members came streaming toward them over the snow. Uncle Webster was dispatched immediately for the doctor, Merriweather hurried upstairs to place hot bricks at the foot of Rosemary's bed, and Mrs. O'Ryan began preparing a posset. Anne and the cousins stripped away Rosemary's chilled garments and dried her briskly with a coarse towel, trying to encourage circulation of the blood. Matilda brought them the flannel nightgown she had been holding close to the fire and they tucked her firmly in, renewing the bricks whenever they began to cool.

During all of this flurry of activity, there had been no sign of life from Rosemary. Her face was pale and her skin clammy, her breathing slow.

"She scarcely seems alive," said Matilda sadly.

"Don't *say* such things," hissed Anne, who was sitting next to Rosemary, wrapping her wet hair in a towel that had been warmed by the fire. "Of course she will be fine once we get her warm enough and she has a chance to rest. That must have been an exhausting experience."

Matilda murmured an apology and started to move away, but Anne reached out and caught her hand, "Forgive me for being such a bear, Matilda. She does look dreadful, doesn't she? Not like Rosemary at all."

She couldn't bring herself to agree completely with what Matilda had said, but Rosemary did look as waxen and still as any corpse she had ever seen.

"I wish Julian were here," she said, half aloud. Although of what help he could be, she had no idea. She merely wanted his comforting presence.

Everyone crept about the house that evening, even the children sitting quietly on the stairs closest to Rosemary's room and watching people go in and out. When Dr. Davis came, he examined her and told them gravely there was nothing he could do for her at this point that they had not already done. "Keep her warm and let her sleep," he said. "And pray that she doesn't contract an inflammation of the lungs." At these dire words, everyone grew pale, for it had been only months ago when they had almost lost Bella to just such an ailment.

Barrisford sat alone in Rosemary's office, unwilling to be where he might have to talk with others. When the door opened suddenly, he looked up with a frown. The newcomer was Julian, and he looked no happier to see Barrisford.

"What were you doing to her that made her skate out on that thin ice?" Julian demanded shortly. "Rosemary knew not to skate out there. She wouldn't have done it if she had been thinking properly. Were you after her again?"

Barrisford looked at him coldly. "You are a fine one to talk about being 'after her,' Melrose."

Julian stared at him. "What are you talking about, Barrisford?"

Barrisford's voice was disdainful. "I am aware that you are her lover," he responded briefly.

"You must have taken a dip in that icy water yourself. Who in thunder told you such a ridiculous tale?" Julian demanded.

"No one needed to tell me. I observed you meeting with her secretly," Barrisford responded.

"Meeting with her sec—" He stopped abruptly and stared at Barrisford. "Just what are you talking about, my lord?"

"I have seen her steal down to the lake to meet you late at night. And I saw you coming downstairs with her in the Swan the other day."

"Well, of course you did, but that doesn't mean that we're lovers. I thought you were supposed to be a clever fellow, Barrisford, but it appears to me that you are not playing with a full deck. If you had seen me with Merriweather on those same occasions, would you have thought that we were lovers?"

Barrisford looked puzzled. "No, of course not, but—"

"There is no 'but' about it, my lord. You have been jumping to conclusions simply because Rosemary is a pretty woman and that is how you think attractive women behave. Rose has told me about your attitude."

Barrisford reddened slightly. "What do you mean, Melrose? What has she told you?"

"That you are not too fond of women, and that you think very highly of your own mental powers and very poorly of those of everyone else. She said it was a shame because there were times when you were almost human."

"'Almost human,'" he murmured. "What a touching tribute." He looked at Julian sharply. "Are you denying that you met her at night on the lake or that you were with her at the Swan?"

"Of course not!" Julian retorted. "Why should I?"

"Then I must continue to think that I was accurate in my estimate of Lady Rosemary's character," responded Barrisford briefly.

Julian clenched his fist and moved toward him. "If you don't beat the Dutch, Barrisford! We can't fight here in Rose's office and create more chaos for her. Step outside with me and we'll settle this now."

"Do sit down and spare me the histrionics, Melrose."

"I'll be dashed if I do! You can't sit there making disparaging comments about the finest girl in the world without my taking exception to it."

"Of course you would think that of her, Melrose. You are in love with her."

Julian stared at him in disbelief. "You are mad, I'll swear that you are, Barrisford! I have *told* you that I am not *in* love with Rose. I love her, yes—dearly, in fact—she is my closest friend. But I am going to marry Anne."

It was Barrisford's turn to look disbelieving. "You are going to marry her sister?" he demanded. "Why had I heard nothing of it?"

"Because *no* one has heard anything of it as yet. I had only just asked her this afternoon and I was going to talk to Rosemary tonight after dinner."

It suddenly came to both of them that not only would Rosemary not be with them after dinner but that there was no assurance she would be with them ever again. There was a brief silence in which Barrisford walked to the fire and stared down into it.

"You were right," Barrisford said abruptly. "The accident was my fault. If I hadn't lost my temper, she would never have made the mistake. I blame myself entirely."

Taken aback by this change of manner, Julian found himself murmuring that Rose had always had a strong constitution and that she was a fighter.

"Yes, I know that she is a fighter," Barrisford said ruefully. "She has shown me that."

He had no desire to continue this conversation or to sit without activity of any kind, allowing his mind to dwell on what might happen. Any action was better than this, and it occurred to him suddenly that he had not seen Aubrey and that the three predators were still at the Hall.

Excusing himself, he went in search of his nephew and found him in the library. As he had feared, Aubrey was seated at a card table with Raxton, Findlay, and Sayers.

"Why are you here, Aubrey, instead of upstairs with Lady Rosemary?" he asked.

"They would not let me stay, Uncle, and I found that the inactivity was beginning to prey upon my nerves. So when these gentlemen invited me to play with them, it seemed to me the reasonable thing to do."

"We thought, Barrisford, that it would help to take his mind off of the situation," interjected Findlay smoothly.

"That was very kind of you," replied Barrisford.

Findlay inclined his head graciously. "We do what we can to be of assistance. We thought that the double onus of discovering that the late duke was still alive and seeing his betrothed in a situation so fraught with peril was too much for him to bear alone."

"Where *is* Stedham?" Barrisford inquired, his attention for the moment deflected from the three gamesters and their victim.

"He went upstairs to check on his daughter.

I daresay that he will be down in just a minute."

Determined to speak to him immediately, Barrisford left the library and went in search of him. He was certain that it would take Findlay and his group more than half an hour to strip Aubrey of his fortune, and so he decided to take care of other matters first.

He encountered Stedham coming back down the stairs. "There has been no change, Barrisford," he said sadly, shaking his head, "And I can't bear to sit there and see how white and still she looks."

"I did not realize that you were so fond of Lady Rosemary, Stedham."

Stedham looked shocked. "Well, after all, Barrisford, she *is* my child—and my eldest at that. When she was born, I was so certain that she would be a boy," he recalled fondly. "But I didn't repine." He sighed deeply. "Still, how different everything would be today *had* she been a boy."

"That is what I would like to speak with you about, Stedham—exactly how everything is today. I was a little surprised to see you on the lake today since I thought your body lay at the bottom of the sea somewhere off the coast of Cornwall."

"Yes, well, so it almost was—or so it might have been—well, actually, Barrisford, I think it would be best if we retired to the library and had a little talk."

"I would very much like that little talk," said Barrisford grimly, "but the library seems to be occupied at the moment."

Stedham looked vaguely surprised for a moment, then nodded. "That's right. They are playing cards in there. You want to have a care, Barrisford, letting your nephew play with those three. I gave him some pointers, but I'm not certain that he will be able to handle them."

"I intend to keep a very close eye on them," responded Barrisford. "And as for your advice to Aubrey, I can only hope devoutly that he does not take it, for your lack of luck with gambling is notorious."

"And that is the root of the problem," agreed Stedham. "Very apt of you to have touched upon it. We'll go to the bookroom and talk it over."

As he opened the door into the bookroom, Barron rose from his place behind the desk, and all three men regarded one another with astonishment.

"Who the devil are you and what are you doing there?" demanded Stedham, incensed by this stranger who was calmly going through ledgers taken from the desk.

"This is Frederick Barron, Lord Stedham," said Barrisford, watching Barron's face with amusement as the name registered. It was obvious that although Barron had heard of Rosemary's accident, he had not heard of the reappearance of her father.

"He was your heir's tutor until Aubrey dismissed him two weeks ago, Stedham," continued Barrisford. "He thought that Barron took too much upon himself."

"I should think so," responded Stedham, swelling with indignation. "If he has dismissed you, sir, then what are you doing here, going through my private papers?"

Barron flushed. "I had thought that Mrs. Townsend would wish for me to—" he began.

"Ha! Amelia Townsend! I should have known that she would come nosing about! Is she *here?*" he asked incredulously.

Barron nodded, edging toward the door.

"Tell her that I'll be up to talk to her about the encroaching ways of her servants, sir! And I wish to see no more of you!"

Barron nodded and shot through the door. Stedham started to follow him, but Barrisford stopped him and indicated a chair by the fire. "We need to talk first, Stedham," he reminded him. "I would like for you to explain to me just how this all came about."

Briefly, Stedham sketched his situation and the arrangements he had made for his "death" while Barrisford listened, fascinated.

"And what of Lady Rosemary?" he inquired. "What did she think of your plan?"

Stedham looked surprised by the question. "Why, what should she think of it, Barrisford?

275

I told her what she must do, and she did it. She knew that otherwise there would be no more Marston Hall, no place for the family to live, no chance of marriage for any of my girls. What could she have done?"

Not having thought of it in just this light, Barrisford began to see that there was a certain point to this line of thinking.

"What about your emerald ring, Stedham? How did that come to be lost?"

Stedham sighed. "I had no money for the ship's captain, so I gave him the ring as a pledge of good faith. He was to hold it for a month. I was certain that by that time, a marriage would have taken place and the dibs would be in tune again and I could give him his money. Unfortunately, he apparently decided that he needed the money right away and took it to a pawnshop. Julian's bailiff saw it and recognized it and Julian gave him the money to come back and reclaim it."

"I see. And Julian gave the ring to Lady Rosemary?"

Stedham nodded. "They didn't want to tell me right away because they were afraid that I would set off to Liverpool to find out what was going on. I wasn't cut out for the quiet life, you see, and staying in the cottage every day was beginning to tell on me."

He thought for a moment. "And then that devil of a sailor from the *Lovely Lady* showed up and scared those two children to death by trying to blackmail them when they didn't have a feather to fly with. I had to send my man Baxter over to the Swan to encourage the fellow to head back to sea on the next available ship."

Barrisford stared at him. "The Swan? That's where the blackmailer was staying?"

Stedham nodded. He looked at Barrisford for a moment and then he added, "Rosemary came to talk to me just before this happened. She seemed to think that my daughter Isabella had grown fond of young Townsend, and that the affection was returned."

Barrisford nodded in agreement. "I think that is probably true," he said.

"Well, I told her we couldn't count on it, and we had to have the money, so she must go through with the marriage. And she said that you had offered for her, but it didn't seem a serious kind of thing and she thought it was just a device to distract her from Townsend. She thought that if she had accepted, you would have left her flat as soon as you had Townsend taken care of.

Barrisford nodded again. "I did make that offer—and I think she's quite right. I think I would have left her just as soon as I had Aubrey in hand again."

"Rosemary is a fair judge of character. I suppose you know that she has been handling business matters here for years."

Barrisford was finding it difficult to stay

seated. He had prided himself on being a canny judge of character, and seldom had he been wider of the mark than he had been with Rosemary.

"Yes, Stedham, so I have heard," he responded. "She is, in fact, a much more apt student of human nature than I am."

There was a brief silence during which Barrisford rose and paced up and down in the tiny office.

"Well, I am properly in the basket now," said Stedham reflectively, staring at the toes of his boots, which were propped against the fender. "But I suppose I will count myself fortunate if I manage to end with all of my family intact."

Barrisford wanted no more conversation with Stedham, and he jerked open the door and strode down the passageway. At least in the great hall there would be enough room to pace at will. When he reached that chamber, however, he found it already occupied. Julian and Anne were under the kissing bough, and it appeared to Barrisford that Anne had most definitely accepted his offer of marriage.

He turned softly so that he would not disturb them, and moved quietly up the stairs so that he could check once more on Rosemary. On the first landing, however, he encountered Aubrey standing with his arms around Isabella.

"What happened to your card game in the library?" he inquired.

"It was really too boring, Uncle, so I excused myself and said that I needed to come check on Rosemary." He suddenly realized that he was still embracing Isabella and he colored slightly but did not release her. "I found Isabella crying and so I felt that I would be more useful here. They will let me do nothing for Rosemary, but at least I can comfort Bella."

"You seem to be doing that quite well," remarked Barrisford. "If you will excuse me, I think that I will see if anything has changed."

"Before you do, Uncle, you might wish to speak with my mother. She is in the drawing room."

"And why would I wish to do something as foolhardy as that, Aubrey?" Barrisford inquired, his eyebrows high.

Aubrey smiled faintly, recognizing a joke of long-standing. They were more likely to warn one another of where she was lying in wait than to encourage the other to seek her out. "She was looking for you earlier, and she has discovered that Lord Stedham is—"

"Alive?" suggested his uncle, smiling.

"Well, yes of course—alive. Have you ever heard of anything stranger?" he asked. "I understand that he was swept overboard and was picked up by a passing ship that couldn't set him down on the English shore immediately.

Isn't it amazing that he should have appeared just at the moment when Rosemary needed him?"

"Astounding," agreed Barrisford dryly. "Did Stedham tell you all of this?"

"No, I haven't really spoken with him about it in all of the confusion. In fact, the only thing he said to me was a bit of advice about how to play my cards. It was Raxton who told me the story."

"Did he indeed?" murmured Barrisford. "An incredible tale. I'm sure that this will be a nine days' wonder in London. Stedham will be in demand at every dinner party of the ton."

He scrutinized Aubrey for a moment. "And what of you, nephew? Does it distress you to no longer be a duke?"

Aubrey laughed. "Not at all. I was beginning to wonder if I should care for all of the duties that attend the title. But I am forever grateful for meeting the Trevelyans." And here he smiled down at Isabella, who attempted a watery smile, but then began to sob into his waistcoat again.

"But we don't know that Rose is going to recover, Aubrey, and if she does, it would be too cruel of us to tell her that you no longer wish to marry her."

"No, of course I must not do so," he agreed seriously. "If she wishes to marry me, I will keep my pledge."

Barrisford extricated a handkerchief for Isabella's use, and said bracingly, "Of course she will recover—and then we shall see how things develop."

"Yes, of course she will be all right. Thank you, my lord."

"We will talk about all of that later. In the meantime, I suppose that I had best find your mother, Aubrey." And leaving the lovers to themselves, he turned back down the stairs, moving silently past Anne and Julian.

"*Robert*, can you *believe* that such an *extraordinary* thing could happen?" demanded Amelia as he entered.

She was dressed all in gold that day, as though to provide the sunshine the winter was lacking.

"It was unbelievable," he agreed sincerely. "What is it that you needed me for, Amelia?"

"Well, to *counsel* us, of course. Now that Stedham is back, I think that we *must* extricate Aubrey from his entanglement with Lady Rosemary."

"Nothing of the sort will be done, Amelia, if they still wish to marry," he replied.

"You cannot be *thinking* properly, Robert! *Do* consider what you are saying."

"And I will add to that," he continued. "If Lady Rosemary and Aubrey should decide not to wed, I strongly suspect that Aubrey would offer for Lady Isabella."

Amelia had been lounging on the sofa, but

when he said this, she sat bolt upright. "You cannot be *serious!* To leave one Trevelyan for *another?* That is a patently *ridiculous* thing to do and I can*not* allow it!"

"I don't believe that you will have anything to say in the matter, Amelia. It will be decided by the parties most nearly concerned." Hearing her continued murmured reproaches, he added, "But if you would be distressed not to have Lady Rosemary as a part of the family, allow me to reassure you. If the opportunity arises, I plan to offer for her myself—although I don't expect her to accept me."

"I *know* that you are *hoaxing* me, Robert, and I do not find it at *all* amusing. You would not *marry* such a creature, and she certainly would not refuse *you*." She paused to take a breath and added, "At any rate, I understand that she *may* not recover from her indisposition—"

She never finished her sentence, for Barrisford rose, his eyes blazing. "She *will* recover, madam, and, although I don't expect to be so fortunate as to have her accept me, I can think of no higher honor should she decide to do so."

Amelia stared at him in astonishment. "Well, I *never* could have believed—"

"You may believe it, Amelia," he said coldly, walking to the door and shutting it behind him.

Merriweather, wreathed in smiles, met him at the door. "She's awake, my lord, and she just drank a little of the posset. Do come in and speak to her for a moment." She stepped aside and then closed the door discreetly behind him.

Rosemary's dark curls were fanned over the pillow in sharp contrast to the whiteness of the linens and of her skin. Her eyes followed him as he approached the bed.

"Why look," she said softly, "it is Sir Galahad, who rescued the lady from the watery grave."

"I came to apologize, Lady Rosemary," he said gravely. "Had it not been for my abominable temper, you would not be lying here now. Because of it, you very nearly had that watery grave."

She started to speak, but he waved her to silence. "No, you must let me say all of this. Having spoken with your father, I know that I was entirely wrong in my estimate of your character, and for that I owe you the profoundest of apologies. I tried to block your wedding, although I had felt at first that Aubrey would be the most fortunate of men to marry you. I feel that way now."

He reached into his waistcoat pocket and pulled out the emerald ring. "I did not give this to your father because I felt that I should return it to you. You were the one from whom I took it."

He took her hand and pressed the ring on her palm, gathering her fingers around it. "I have a rare talent for spoiling happiness, my lady. From first to last, my behavior to you has been unforgivable. I wish you very happy in your life with Aubrey." And he turned to leave the room.

"Lord Barrisford," she called softly, just before he reached the door. "Do you still have your charm from the Christmas pudding?"

He looked at her blankly and shook his head. "No, I did not keep it. I believe I left it at the table that evening."

She smiled gently at him, taking the small gold ring from an enameled box on her bedside table and handed it to him.

"Are you terribly wealthy, Lord Barrisford?" she inquired, her eyes dancing.

He nodded.

"As rich as Golden Ball?"

"Richer," Barrisford responded soberly.

She stared at him for a moment, as though thinking deeply. Then she smiled again and spoke with the air of one conferring a great favor. "Then you may marry me, Lord Barrisford." And she extended her hand for the small gold ring from the pudding.

"Even though I am domineering and occasionally bad-tempered?" he inquired, taking her hand and slipping the trinket onto her finger.

She nodded. "You must remember, my lord, that I am marrying you for your money. I understand that you respect honesty."

"Will I be browbeaten?" he demanded.

She nodded firmly. "Undoubtedly. That will be vital if I am to keep you from grinding me into the earth whenever I disagree with you."

"And will you give me a proper setdown whenever I deserve it?"

"Most definitely," she assured him. "Perhaps even when you do not deserve it."

Both parties appeared to find this a highly satisfactory arrangement, and Barrisford, seating himself on the side of the bed in a most improper manner, gathered her carefully to him and kissed her, surrendering himself wholeheartedly to a new love and a new life. Downstairs the young lovers made their plans and in the drawing room Amelia had fallen prey to the Trevelyan charm and was listening avidly to Stedham's miraculous return from the dead. In the library the three gamesters, surrounded by an interested audience of the cousins and most of the children, had found themselves reduced to a game of silver loo for penny stakes and mugs of apple cider.

In the kitchen Candace, with Annie Laurie and two of the pups in her lap, was talking with Uncle Webster and Mrs. O'Ryan. "All things considered," she said judiciously, with the air of a connoisseur, "this has been a most extraordinary—but satisfactory—Christmas." Annie Laurie appeared to agree with her, for she sprang from her lap like a thing possessed and raced three times around the edge of the kitchen, dodging legs and children and leaping stools, ending finally in a tangle of legs at Candace's feet. Leaning down to scratch the terrier's ears, Candace hummed the refrain of her favorite carol:

Love and joy come to you,
And to you your wassail too,
And God bless you, and send you
  A happy New Year,
And God send you a happy New Year.

A Memorable Collection of Regency Romances

BY ANTHEA MALCOLM AND VALERIE KING

THE COUNTERFEIT HEART   (3425, $3.95/$4.95)
by Anthea Malcolm

Nicola Crawford was hardly surprised when her cousin's betrothed disappeared on some mysterious quest. Anyone engaged to such an unromantic, but handsome man was bound to run off sooner or later. Nicola could never entrust her heart to such a conventional, but so deucedly handsome man. . . .

THE COURTING OF PHILIPPA   (2714, $3.95/$4.95)
by Anthea Malcolm

Miss Philippa was a very successful author of romantic novels. Thus she was chagrined to be snubbed by the handsome writer Henry Ashton whose own books she admired. And when she learned he considered love stories completely beneath his notice, she vowed to teach him a thing or two about the subject of love. . . .

THE WIDOW'S GAMBIT   (2357, $3.50/$4.50)
by Anthea Malcolm

The eldest of the orphaned Neville sisters needed a chaperone for a London season. So the ever-resourceful Livia added several years to her age, invented a deceased husband, and became the respectable Widow Royce. She was certain she'd never regret abandoning her girlhood until she met dashing Nicholas Warwick. . . .

A DARING WAGER   (2558, $3.95/$4.95)
by Valerie King

Ellie Dearborne's penchant for gaming had finally led her to ruin. It seemed like such a lark, wagering her devious cousin George that she would obtain the snuffboxes of three of society's most dashing peers in one month's time. She could easily succeed, too, were it not for that exasperating Lord Ravenworth. . . .

THE WILLFUL WIDOW   (3323, $3.95/$4.95)
by Valerie King

The lovely young widow, Mrs. Henrietta Harte, was not all inclined to pursue the sort of romantic folly the persistent King Brandish had in mind. She had to concentrate on marrying off her penniless sisters and managing her spendthrift mama. Surely Mr. Brandish could fit in with her plans somehow . . .